™ & © 2007 Sony Pictures Animation, Inc. All rights reserved.

HarperCollins®, ≛®, and HarperEntertainment™ are trademarks of
HarperCollins Publishers.
Printed in the U.S.A.

For information address HarperCollins Children's Books, a division of
HarperCollins Publishers, 1350 Avenue of the Americas, New York, NY 10019.
Library of Congress catalog card number: 2007921505
www.harpercollinschildrens.com
www.surfsup.com
ISBN-13: 978-0-06-115332-7 — ISBN-10: 0-06-115332-X
Book design by Joe Merkel
❖
First Edition

THE LIFE
AND TIMES OF
CODY MAVERICK

BY SUSAN KORMAN

HARPERENTERTAINMENT
AN IMPRINT OF HARPERCOLLINSPUBLISHERS

CHAPTER 1

HeY, DUDe! NiCe tO Meet YOU!

My name is Cody Maverick, and I'm a movie star!

Okay . . . Well, actually, I'm not *really* like a big movie star or anything. . . . I'm a surfer. But last year these pretty famous film guys were making a movie about an "up-and-coming surfer," and they wanted me to be the star of it. They came all the way to Shiverpool, Antarctica, so that they could film me doing my thing.

Wait. You've never heard of a penguin from Antarctica who surfs? Really?

I admit it's pretty unusual. And plenty of penguins, including my own mom, think I'm weird—way different from all the other penguins in Shiverpool. But I've been surfing since I was little. In fact, ever since that day when I met Big Z Topanga and—

1

What? What's that?

Did you say, "Who's Big Z?"

Oh, man. Get serious! You really don't know about Big Z?

He's hard core, dude! The greatest surfer who ever lived! They invented the ocean just for him!

Sorry, I don't mean to get all carried away or anything; it's just that Big Z is everything. He's basically the heart of the whole surfing movie.

His real name is Zeke "Big Z" Topanga, and back in the sixties, he ruled the sport of surfing. I was just a little kid when he came to Antarctica on a surfing tour. Man, when he came cruising into Shiverpool on a whale that day, it was the biggest thing that had ever happened in my hometown.

Suddenly, there he was. Just floating over the water, hovering, you know, as if he were weightless or something.

Everybody ran down to the beach to see him. I was so excited, I pushed my way to the front of the crowd.

And you know what?

He could have walked up to anyone that day. But he walked right up to me. And then he gave me this— an awesome, one-of-a-kind Big Z necklace.

Here. Want to see it? It's got a shell with a big Z carved into it. I wear it every single day.

After he gave it to me, you know what he said?

He told me, "Kid, no matter what, find a way. 'Cause that's what winners do. They find a way."

That's what winners do. . . . They find a way.

I'll never forget those words.

Big Z was the greatest, man. Everyone looked up to him, respected him, loved him. And that day when he stopped in Shiverpool, I made a promise to myself: One day I was going to be just like him.

Is Big Z still around? Is that what you want to know?

Whew . . . Tough question.

I guess you never saw it on TV . . . ? The clip of that day when he . . . when that monster wave crashed down and . . .

Oh, wow.

You know what I'm thinking, dude? You'd better grab a seat. And then if I were you, I'd find some tissues, too.

Because what happened to Big Z is a long, sad story.

CHAPTER 2

WHEN THE GUYS MAKING THE MOVIE

first came to Shiverpool, they asked me, "Why do you surf?"

And I said, "Look around, man."

My mom is always asking me the same thing, and like I tell her, I surf because I have to surf. It's the one piece of joy that I have.

I don't know if you've ever been to Shiverpool, but let me tell you, it's a pretty depressing place. You've got your barren ice fields, gigantic icebergs, and, oh, your frigid winds blasting about one hundred miles an hour every single day.

You get the picture, right?

When I brought the film crew to the fish pile, they understood even better.

I mean, who wants to work all day long, sorting

mackerel from herring? It's the dumbest thing I've ever heard of. But I had to do it, just to keep my mom off my back about the surfing, you know what I mean?

I showed the film crew my house, too. It's one of the igloos along the shore—the one with all the ice surfboards leaning there. That's where I grew up with my mom and my brother, Glen. It's just the three of us, and I've always been known as the "little" brother in the family. Ask my mom. She tells everyone that I was the little, teeny, small egg, and Glen was the great big one.

Glen can't stand that I surf either. He's an egg hatcher right now. His job is to sit on eggs all day long out in the cold.

Of course he had plenty to say about me to the filmmakers.

"Cody's out there in the water all day, you know, shirking his responsibilities. He doesn't get it, man. He needs to step up and be a man."

That's all I ever hear from him. How I'm shirking my responsibilities by following my crazy dreams by surfing.

You and I know there's more to life than hatching eggs. But Glen doesn't realize that.

What's that? Oh . . . my dad . . . ?

To tell you the truth, I don't really like to talk about it.

He, er . . . It was an orca whale attack.

I don't really remember him. But I've always thought—maybe it's crazy—but I've always thought that things might have been a little different if my dad were still around.

I mean, I know my mom loves me and all, but she doesn't get the whole surfing thing. And when Glen and everybody else in Shiverpool says, "Cody's a bum, Cody's this, Cody's that," she gets kind of judgmental about it, too.

That's why I've always had dreams. Dreams about becoming a pro surfer and getting away from Shiverpool for good.

And luckily for me, there was someone out there who knew how to make surfers' dreams come true.

Have you ever heard of Reggie Belafonte?

No?

He's a sea otter who has this crazy hairdo, and he organizes surfing contests and tours and stuff like that.

When the film crew went to interview Reggie for the surfing flick, he was doing what Reggie does: sitting around in a hot tub eating oysters. Meanwhile, all these penguins were fluttering around him, fixing his hair and bringing him fancy coconut drinks.

Of course he wanted to tell the moviemakers only about himself.

"I find these kids, I bring them here, and you know what I do? I give them a chance to be somebody."

And then he took credit for Big Z's success.

"You know I made Big Z, right? Before me he was just another surfer."

Pen Gu Island, where Reggie lives, is basically the surfing capital of the world. And around this time it was really busy because the Tenth Annual Big Z Memorial Surf-Off was coming up.

Have you heard of that?

That's right. It is the biggest surfing contest around.

A lot of surfers were already there, getting ready to compete.

SPEN—Sporting Penguin Entertainment Network— was camped out there, too, broadcasting everything.

"From near and far, water birds are flocking here to compete in the largest surf contest in the world," an announcer said into a microphone. He turned to the two former pros standing with him. "Kelly, Rob, tell us what we can expect when this contest begins in just a few days."

"Thanks, Sal," Kelly said. She gestured at a huge wave behind her. "The locals call this wave 'Po Chu,' the crusher. It's totally beautiful from where I'm standing, but even the pros are going to think twice before paddling into this monster."

The SPEN camera cut to Rob. He pointed down to the end of the beach, where jagged rocks sliced through the ocean's surface. "Not only that, this tricky right swell ends the rocky reef known as the Boneyards, made infamous by Big Z. All in all, it's a huge challenge for the competitors."

"And as if that weren't enough," the announcer chimed in, "our surfers will be facing off against Tank 'the Shredder' Evans. Tank is the nine-time defending champ."

I'll tell you more about Tank later. But let me sum him up now this way: The guy is a total jerk.

Even though the contest was coming up fast, Reggie B. still had his talent scouts out, scouring the globe for the next big thing.

And this, my friend, is where I enter the picture.

Get it . . . *picture*? And we're talking about a movie? Pretty clever, huh?

CHAPTER 3

I was back in shiverpool working

on the fish pile on day 78 of Reggie Belafonte's Global Recruiting Tour. The tour whale cruised into town past the icebergs and headed for the beach. Standing on the whale's back was Mikey Abromowitz, the shore bird who was Reggie's main talent scout.

Mikey had already been to Japan, Australia, Brazil, and a million other places around the world. He wasn't exactly thrilled to be in Shiverpool, let me tell you. Icicles hung from his beak, and a scowl was frozen on his face.

"Reggie doesn't look for new talent," he muttered under his breath as he disembarked. "*I* do. *I* find these penguins. And the stress is killing me."

He started walking around Shiverpool. "Excuse me! Excuse me!" He skittered through a crowd of penguins

9

on his little chopstick legs. "Does anybody in this entire frozen wasteland surf?"

One of the old geezer penguins answered him. "That Cody Maverick kid does."

"Wonderful . . . ," Mikey muttered.

I was at the top of the fish pile when Mikey showed up.

"I'm looking for . . . uh . . . I'm looking for Cody Maverick," I heard somebody say. "Has anyone seen Cody Maverick?"

"I'm Cody Maverick," I called down.

"Terrific," Mikey said, even though it sounded as if he couldn't care less. "I'm Mikey Abromowitz from the Big Z Memorial Surf-Off, Pen Gu Island."

"The Big Z Memorial Surf-Off . . . ?" I echoed. Then it dawned on me. "You came here on the whale! Wow! You came here to see me!"

I tossed the fish I was holding and slid down the slippery pile to shake his hand.

Mikey lifted his eyebrows. "You're quite a slip and slider, aren't you?"

I was so excited, I could barely get out any words. "You're here . . . I can't . . . What an honor, sir . . . ," I fumbled. "Honestly, it's quite an honor!"

"Lovely. Wonderful," Mikey said, sounding bored.

"So I hear you, uh, surf? Is this true?"

"Oh yeah, man, I surf," I said. "You gotta see what I can do."

"Really?" Mikey snapped a few icicles off his beak and looked at me doubtfully. "You mean you can actually stand on a surfboard?"

"Oh yeah!" I had to get one of my ice-boards before this guy took off. "I'll be right back! You're gonna see what I can do, and then you're gonna be happy and everything's gonna be good, and I'm coming with you!"

Mikey rolled his eyes as I ran off to my igloo. "I can't imagine a better day . . . ," he muttered sarcastically.

Mom was chopping fish in the kitchen when I burst in.

"Ma—Ma—the scout—Mikey! He came! He's here!" I shouted.

Mom came to the door. "What?"

"He's giving me a shot in the Big Z Surf-Off, Mom! You've got to watch me!"

She sighed. "That's okay, Cody."

"Just this time? Please?"

"I'm busy, Cody. Can't you see that I'm in the middle of chopping fish?"

I had to let it go. "Okay. All right," I called over my shoulder. "Well, wish me luck."

"Good luck," she murmured.

I grabbed a board and raced toward Shiverpool Beach. Mikey watched from shore as I threw the board in the water and paddled out.

Dude, I'm telling you. It was my worst nightmare.

There were absolutely no waves. The ocean was as still as a pond.

A pond!

"Any time now!" Mikey yelled impatiently.

I didn't know what to do. This was my big chance and I couldn't surf at all.

"You should've been here yesterday!" I shouted to him. "We had a sweet swell. I mean, I was doing some layback 360s and floaters. . . . It was insane!"

"Wow!" Mikey faked excitement. Then he turned toward where the whale was waiting for him. "Start the whale. We're taking off."

I shot out of the water.

"No! No! No-no-no-no! Wait! Wait! Wait! Just give me one more chance. All I need is one chance!" I begged him.

But Mikey was heartless. "You just had your one chance, buddy."

I dropped to my knees on the icy beach. "Please! Dude! Please don't go! There were no waves!"

"Tough break, kid," Mikey said. "Better luck next year!"

My dreams were shattering right in front of my eyes. "No . . . no . . . no . . . Hold on! Wait!" I cried. "Just one sec!"

Mikey hopped onto the whale's fin and ran up its side. "Let's go. . . . Let's go. . . . Let's go . . . ," he told his crew. "That kid is coming. . . . Let's go. . . ."

I reached the whale just as it left shore. "Oh, man . . . ," I murmured, running a fin through my hair.

Can you believe it?

I had just missed the boat to the Big Z Memorial Surf-Off.

CHAPTER 4

I STOOD THERE WATCHING THE BOAT

cruise away from Shiverpool. Suddenly, I could hear Big Z's voice in my ear.

"You know, kid, no matter what, find a way. 'Cause that's what winners do."

I could not let this chance get away from me.

I grabbed my board and raced into the water. "Hold on!" I shouted. A minute later, I was cutting through the whale's massive wake. "Wait up! I'm coming to Pen Gu!"

Mikey stood on top of the whale, scowling at me. "No way, no how!" he shouted. "This is a contest for *big wave surfers*!" Then he jumped up and down on the whale's back. "Can't this blubber ball go any faster? Step on it, fish sticks!"

The whale slammed its fluke down onto the water, right on top of me.

"No!" I shrieked, too late. "No! No! No!" My ice-board had shattered into a million pieces.

Mikey stared down at the broken bits of ice floating in the water.

"Poor kid," he murmured to some of the surfers he'd already recruited. "I feel a little bad about this. Honestly, it's embarrassing."

"No, wait, Mikey! Wait!" I'd gotten hold of the whale's fluke—that's how determined I was.

The surprised whale lifted me high into the air and drew back his tail. Then he flipped me back at least a mile, sending me skipping across the water like a tiny stone.

"Whoa . . . ," Mikey murmured. "That didn't look too good."

A minute later, I was back at them, swimming through the water like a porpoise. *"Waaaaiiiiiitttt!"* I screamed.

I caught up to the whale and grabbed his side. By now the other surfers were cheering me on.

"Go, kid!" they shouted. "Go!"

I scrambled frantically up the side of the whale. But it was so slick, I couldn't hold on.

"Help!" I yelled desperately. "I can't—"

Just then something dropped down next to me.

It was a surfboard, a small surfboard, shaped exactly like an ear of corn.

Yep, you heard me all right—it was shaped like an ear of corn.

I grabbed hold.

"We got you!" someone shouted.

I looked up. A chicken—yes, a chicken—was hoisting me up.

"We got you!" the chicken called. "Oh! You're heavier than you look!"

With all his might, he dragged me onto the top of the whale.

I collapsed, exhausted.

"Whoo! Man, we did it! Teamwork always pays off, man!" said the chicken.

I was really out of breath. "Thank . . . you . . . ," I panted. "Thank you so much. . . ."

"I'm Chicken Joe," he introduced himself. "Dude, I've never seen anyone rip up a wave like that, man! How'd you do that?"

I grinned at him. "Thanks."

"Joe!" Mikey called.

"That was some sweet board you were riding," Chicken Joe went on. "What was it made of? Ice?"

"Joe! Hey, Joe!"

For some reason Mikey was trying to get Chicken Joe's attention. Finally, he dangled a corn on the cob in front of him like a hypnotist.

"*Bwuck . . . Bwuck . . . ,*" Chicken Joe murmured sleepily.

Mikey hurled the corn on the cob off to the side, and Chicken Joe chased after it.

"I want to talk to you, Maverick."

I gulped as Mikey turned to me.

"Don't you ever, ever do anything like that in the contest—all right?"

"What?! Did you say, in the contest? Does that mean I'm in?"

"Yeah, you're in," Mikey replied. "Because your ride was entertaining, in a horrifying kind of way."

I was so happy, I wanted to hug him. Instead, I just gave him a wave and then pulled myself up onto the deck. And when I looked back toward the shore at Shiverpool, I couldn't see it anymore. My hometown had already faded into the fog.

CHAPTER 5

Have you ever been to Pen Gu Island?

No?

Well, let me tell you—it is the most beautiful tropical paradise you can imagine. There are tall palm trees, beaches with perfect white sand, and best of all, the water is crystal blue with enormous swells.

Joe and I gazed at the island as the whale drew closer.

"Man, these waves are nothing like Lake Michigan," Chicken Joe said.

"Lake Michigan?" I echoed. "You mean you can actually surf on a lake?"

He nodded. "Oh yeah, man. Totally!"

Mikey started waking up the other surfers. "Okay, everyone! Get ready to disembark."

18

Chicken Joe instantly took off, walking toward the edge of the whale.

"No, Joe!" I warned him. "No!"

But it was too late. He slipped down the side of the whale and splashed into the ocean.

"Hey, nobody panic, but this island is completely surrounded by water!" Chicken Joe joked.

Mikey sighed. "Would somebody please help the chicken?"

We all stepped onshore a few minutes later, including the camera crew that was following me around.

A pretty gentoo penguin greeted me and put a lei around my neck. "Welcome to Pen Gu," she said with a warm smile.

Someone else handed me a colorful drink. Nearby, vendors in huts sold souvenirs and different kinds of food and tropical drinks.

Surfers—and surfboards—lined the beach. As I looked around, I spotted a big penguin showing his biceps to a group of girls.

I turned to the movie guys. "That's Tank Evans!" I exclaimed. "He's huge!"

Then I saw something else on the beach—a set of concrete footprints marked BIG Z.

"Dudes!" I waved the filmmakers over. "Check it out! I'm standing where Z stood. Get a shot of me here!"

Chicken Joe was busy sampling all the food. "Cody, you gotta try this stuff! It's called squid on a stick."

I looked over and let out a laugh. He was dressed in a hula skirt and a wig, with dozens of leis and necklaces draped over his neck.

I wasn't into the squid on a stick. "No, I'm okay," I told him.

"Come on, just one bite!"

"All right. One bite, that's it." I took a small bite.

"Well, what do you think?"

"Not bad . . . ," I told him. "I mean, it kind of tastes like chick—" I stopped myself in the nick of time.

Chicken Joe looked at me. "What? What do you mean, 'chick' . . . ?"

Luckily, a lifeguard—a girl lifeguard—raced past us just then.

"Coming through!" she called loudly. "Coming through!"

Oh, man. She was petite with big blue eyes and really soft-looking feathers. I couldn't help it. I stood there like an idiot, staring at her.

Suddenly, she stopped in her tracks and looked back at me. "Oh, shoot!" she burst out. "I forgot something."

Then she whirled around and ran back past me again. She reappeared in a second with a flotation device.

"Wow . . . ," I murmured, watching her dash into the water. "I think I'm in love."

In the water, a little kid was yelling and flapping his fins.

"Help me! I'm drowning!"

"I'm coming, Arnold!" the cute lifeguard called back. "Don't panic!"

We watched her pull the little kid out of the water in, like, two seconds. She was amazing at her job.

Chicken Joe nudged me. "Well, what are you standing here next to me for? Go talk to her, man."

I shook my head. "No. I can't talk to her!"

Still, I inched closer.

"You're okay, Arnold," I heard her saying to the little kid she'd just rescued. "You'll be fine."

"Thank you, Lani." He gave her a little smile.

"But this is the third time you've gone unconscious this week," she went on. "I just don't think it's very good for your brain."

"I know." The boy sounded sheepish. "I'll see you later, Lani. Bye." He waddled away.

Chicken Joe pushed me toward her. *"Go!"*

"Stop it, Joe!" I hissed at him.

But I was already face to face with her. She stood there staring at me with a funny look on her face.

"Uh . . . uhhh . . ." I stammered. "That was awesome how you, er, saved that kid's life and all. That was just unbelievable, really."

"Hmmm-hmmm," Lani replied.

"Yeah," I said awkwardly.

At least she knew how to make conversation. "So, are you here for the surf contest?"

"Uhhh . . . mmmm . . . hmmm . . . ," I managed to reply.

"I'll be watching you," she said.

My heart did this little thump thing. "Really? You'll be watching me?"

"Well, yeah," she went on. "From the lifeguard station. It's my job."

"Oh. . . . right. . . . That's your job," I murmured.

"Hey, Cody!" Chicken Joe yelled suddenly. "What's going on? Are you gonna kiss her or what?"

My face turned bright red. I grabbed Chicken Joe by the neck before he could blurt out something else.

"C'mon, Joe! We've got a lot to do."

"Dude," he argued, "you were the one saying you were in love with her!" He looked back at Lani. "He really digs you!"

My face turned a million shades of red again. "Joe! Shhh!"

I couldn't see her reaction. I was too busy trying to drag Chicken Joe away before he embarrassed me some more.

CHAPTER 6

CHICKEN JOE AND I WALKED ALONG

the beach later, still talking about Lani.

"Just lay some feeling on her," Chicken Joe told me.

"What do you mean, 'lay some feeling on her'?"

"You know, through your words, through—"

"Whoa!" I came to an abrupt halt. In the middle of a sharp reef in the water, a battered surfboard lay propped up on a rock. Brightly colored flowers were strewn along the bottom of the board.

"What's that?" Chicken Joe asked.

I had recognized it right away. "It's Big Z's shrine!" I told him. "That's it!"

"Whooooaaa," Chicken Joe breathed. "Awesome!"

I had seen the shrine dozens of times on TV. But it was different seeing it in person, right in front of my face.

As I stared at the beat-up board in the center of the shrine, I remembered seeing pictures of it lying in pieces on this same beach. I could still hear the TV announcer's grave voice:

"Big Z took his final ride this morning during a competition with up-and-coming surfer Tank Evans." On TV they showed Z paddling into a giant wave and then riding down its face. The next thing anybody knew the wave had crashed down on Z, and he was . . .

He was gone.

I told you to grab some tissues, didn't I?

"Z was last seen paddling off into a massive swell off Pen Gu Bay," the announcer went on. "That means Tank Evans is surfing's new champion."

At a ceremony, the other surfers gathered in the water on their boards and threw leis into the ocean. Then they'd created this amazing shrine to remember Big Z.

"I'll never forget that day he came to Shiverpool," I told Chicken Joe. "Big Z changed my life. He really did."

Thud. Thud.

Somebody was throwing rocks at the shrine. I looked up. It was that monster Tank Evans.

"Hey!" I cried. "Cut it out!"

"He's got a pretty good throwing fin," Chicken Joe murmured.

"Stop that!" I shouted. "What are you doing?"

Tank kept on throwing rocks, nailing Big Z's board every time.

"Whoa!" Chicken Joe said. "That's like three in a row!"

I ran over to Tank. "I said, cut it out!"

Tank laughed and threw me a stone. "Here. Give it a shot."

I was going to give it a shot, all right. I wound up and threw the stone—right at Tank's head.

I told you I could surf, but I never said anything about being smart.

Tank let out a scary-sounding growl. Then he stomped over and got right in my face. Just when I thought he was about to punch me, he noticed something on my neck.

"Oh, look at that! He's got jewelry. It's, a . . ." He picked up my necklace. " . . . a Big Z necklace. Oh, this is priceless!"

He yanked hard on the necklace, pulling me closer to him.

"Stop it!" I shouted. "Let go!"

People around us on the beach began to sense a

fight. They circled us.

"Big Z," Tank sneered. "He's a Big Zero."

"You don't deserve to talk about him like that!" I shot back. "Shut your mouth!"

"Zero. It starts with a Z!"

"You will never be as good as Big Z, *Stank*!" I shot back.

"Oooooh!" somebody gasped. "Did you hear that? He called him *Stank*!"

"Hey, hey, people." Chicken Joe stepped between us, trying to make peace. "Come on now, smile on your brother!"

Tank shoved Chicken Joe to the ground. "Keep your girlfriend out of this!" he snarled at me.

"You can't do that to my friend!" Furious, I reached over and punched him.

"Nice. Nice." Tank just laughed as I kept on punching him. "Why don't you work the lats a little bit while you're there?" He turned around so I could punch his backside. "Here, why don't you get a little bit of the glutes, too? There you go."

After he'd gotten his little laugh from the crowd, he reached over and grabbed someone's surfboard and held it over my head.

Before Tank could flatten me with it, Reggie

Belafonte pushed his way between us. "Hey, hey, hey! Whoa! Whoa! Whoa! All right. That's enough, guys."

Not for me.

"I'll take you on anytime, anywhere!" I told Tank.

You could almost see the lightbulb go on over Reggie's head.

He looked toward the crowd, a sly smile on his face. "All right! Who wants to see this little guy take on the champ?"

People started cheering.

"Kill Tank!" a kid yelled. I think it might have been Arnold, the little guy who Lani had saved.

Reggie was busy pumping up the crowd. "Ladies and gentlemen, today we're bringing you a little one-on-one surfing action between Tank Evans and . . . er, Jerry—"

"Cody!" I reminded him. "It's Cody."

"Cody Maverick," Mikey chimed in.

"Cody Mavenkirk!" Reggie blared. "And the one who rides the biggest wave wins!"

At that, the fans cheered and started chanting our names.

When Mikey handed me a surfboard, my stomach did a wild 360 thing.

Oh, man, I thought, looking at Tank, who was already strutting down the beach with his board. I wasn't even in the water yet. So why did I feel like I was in way over my head?

CHAPTER 7

TANK EVANS AND I PADDLED OUT

into the deep water side by side. Along the way, I spotted some scary-looking spiny sea urchins.

Oh, and did I mention? This part of the water had plenty of pointy, jagged rocks sticking up everywhere.

I mean, I was used to surfing around sharp icebergs on Antarctica. But this was different—way different.

Even the film crew looked a little worried for me.

"So, Cody," a camera guy called, "are you nervous about going up against Tank Evans?"

"What?" I pretended I couldn't hear.

He repeated the question.

"Nervous?" I echoed, giving a fake little laugh. "What do I have to be nervous about?" The guy didn't bother to answer. He just filmed me paddling up a wave so big, it was going to make me look like an ant on camera. I barely made it over the top.

Still, I have to say: It seemed like the crowd was rooting for me. I could hear them chanting my name from the shore, "Co-dee! Co-dee!"

Tank and I were in the water side by side, waiting for the right wave.

"I'm gonna chum the water with your head!" he snarled.

"Bring it on!" I shouted back.

On the horizon a wave was building fast.

"It's mine!" we both shouted, furiously steering our boards toward it. "I'm taking that one!"

As I paddled out, I could hear my own voice in my head, replaying what I'd said to the filmmakers the other day.

"*So when you take the first wave, Cody, and the whole island's watching, what's that going to be like?*"

"*It's gonna be amazing! Honestly, it's gonna be the best wave of my life, and I hope the cameras are rolling, 'cause you're gonna want to watch it over and over and over again. . . .*"

Suddenly I wasn't so sure about that.

Paddling like mad, I caught the wave just right. I hopped up on my board. And then . . .

The wave exploded over me. I fell off the board and

plunged down into the water.

Way, way down.

On the shore, the spectators cringed. "Ooohhh . . ."

"Poor kid. Poor kid," Mikey kept saying.

But Reggie had a different attitude. "That was spectacular! What a wipeout!"

The white water tossed me around like a sock inside a washing machine. I fought to get to the surface. But, just as I tried to take a breath, another wave pounded me, driving me down onto the reef.

Somewhere around then, I went unconscious, and the rest is all a blur.

I do know, though, that Lani raced into the water to rescue me. She quickly grabbed hold of me and dragged me back to shore.

Overhead, the sky had turned dark. Thunder sounded in the distance while Lani frantically gave me CPR. "Come on . . . come on . . . come on . . . ," she said again and again.

Chicken Joe rushed over. "Can I help? I can help. Except if there's blood. Blood just makes me want to—"

Woozy from thinking about blood, Chicken Joe fainted.

"Somebody help the chicken!" Lani yelled at the crowd.

A second later, I came to.

"Did I win?" I asked, coughing. "I won, right?"

Mikey dragged my surfboard across the sand. "I told you to stay in Antarctica, kid," he muttered. "But nobody ever listens to me."

I lay on the sand on my back. "Oh, wow . . . ," I said in a goofy voice. "There are pixies everywhere."

"You're fine, Cody." I could kind of hear Lani's voice. "You're going to be okay. It's all right. . . ."

Thunder boomed.

And then I blacked out again.

CHAPTER 8

I WAS STILL OUT COLD WHEN LANI

scooped me up and threw me onto her back. It was dark and raining hard as she carried me through the dense jungle for miles.

Who knew that a penguin her size could be so strong?

Finally, she came to an enormous, weird-looking banyan tree. Its vines formed windows and a front door.

Poor Lani was about to collapse from carrying me for so long.

"Hey, Geek! Geek!" she called out breathlessly.

Gazing around, she spotted someone sleeping in a hammock. It was a large, overweight penguin with broken feathers hanging in his face like dreadlocks. As he snored loudly, rainwater filled up his beak.

"Figures . . . ," Lani muttered.

She went over to the hammock and gazed sadly at the penguin.

Then, without warning, she shoved him out of the hammock.

"Geek! Wake up!" she cried. "Wake up!"

"Oh, man . . ." Geek was groggy as he struggled to get up. "Lani."

"I need your help," Lani said. "Come on. Get off your lazy butt and come and help me."

"Lani . . ." Geek shook his head. "I was having this beautiful dream about—"

"Geek! I don't care." She turned to carry me inside the tree.

"Wait!" Geek was suddenly wide awake. "Wait! Wait! Wait!"

"What?" Lani said impatiently.

"Who is that guy?" Geek demanded, his eyes on me.

"He's a surfer," Lani explained. "He's hurt."

Then Geek spotted the camera crew.

"Who are all those guys?"

"They're with this guy, and if you help—"

"Lani!" Geek cut her off. "What are you doing?"

"If you help him, they'll go away," she said, disappearing inside the tree with me.

35

"Oh, man . . ." Geek ran a fin through the broken feathers hanging down in his face. Then he picked up a bunch of rocks and spun toward the camera crew. "Get out of here!" he yelled, hurling the rocks right at the camera lens. He stomped inside behind Lani.

She was looking around, trying to figure out a place to dump me.

Geek's house was a total mess. I mean, I'm a slob and everything, but his place . . . Garbage was everywhere. A table was strewn with old food—fish bones, clamshells, and dirty coconut cups. Strange abstract drawings decorated the walls.

"Where do you want him, Geek?" Lani asked.

Geek wasn't feeling very hospitable. "Nowhere!" he snapped. "That's the whole point!"

Lani cleared off the table and gently lay me down.

"No outsiders!" Geek reminded her. "Come on now, Lani, I've told you this—"

"I know! I know!" she cut him off. "But—"

"No outsiders," Geek repeated.

"This is an emergency, Geek," Lani pleaded. "He went down bad right over the falls. I don't even know if he, uhh . . ."

Her words trailed off when she saw what Geek was looking at—my Big Z necklace.

"Geek," Lani murmured. "Please."

He groaned and then tossed aside the necklace and began to examine me.

"His breathing is weak," he said, bending over my chest. "And his pulse is way down. Hmmm. Did he hit the reef?"

"I'm not sure," Lani admitted. "I got to him after he . . ."

"Whoa, whoa, whoa, whoa," Geek cut her off, holding up my foot.

"Here's the answer: He *definitely* hit the reef." He pulled out a long red spine from the bottom of my foot.

"Owww!" I jerked awake. "Ohhh!!"

"Cody!" Lani said, relieved. "You're okay!"

I winced. "I hurt all over."

"You're going to be okay," Lani reassured me.

"I don't know about that," Geek chimed in, frowning. "This is pretty bad. In fact, it's really bad."

"What?" Lani demanded.

Geek pointed to the long, mean-looking spine he'd removed. "This is from a fire urchin." He peered more closely at it. "Actually, it's amazing."

I didn't know what he was talking about. "What's amazing?"

"That you're still alive!" Geek told me. "Do you know how much poison's in one of these suckers?"

"No . . ." I felt as if I were going to pass out again.

"It's all right," Geek went on. "I can fix you up just fine."

In the candlelight I could see a worried expression on Lani's face.

"You're not going to . . ." Her words trailed off ominously.

Now I was really worried. "He's not going to what?" I demanded.

Geek walked over to a medicine chest and began sorting through the stuff inside.

"Do you want him to lose his foot?" Geek said to Lani. She shook her head.

"Then hold him down," Geek ordered.

I watched him rummage through the medicine chest, pulling out scary-looking stuff: a sharp shell, something that looked like pliers. . . . When he picked up a sawfish saw, I really freaked out.

"Keep that crazy witch doctor away from me!" I tried to scramble off the table.

Lani held me down. "It's all right, Cody, he's not a real doctor."

"What?" Now I was totally panicked. "Let me go!"

"Hurry, Geek!" Lani struggled to keep me there.

"Geek?" Suddenly, I clued in on the guy's name. "What kind of name is Geek?"

Neither one answered. Instead, Geek was talking away to himself like a crazy person. "Where'd it go?" he murmured. "I just saw it the other day. . . . Ah, here we go. . . ."

He found what he'd been looking for. He reached in and pulled out a gourd.

Then he pulled a cork out of a hole in the gourd and swigged something down. "Water!" he announced, flinging it away. "Just what I needed!"

He shook his arms like a boxer going into the ring and stepped toward me.

My heart thumped like a drum. "No . . . please . . ."

He ignored me. "All right. Come on. Let's do this, Lani. Hold him down."

I flailed about like crazy, but she was too strong for me.

"Relax, okay?" Geek said to me. "You've been stung, man, and this is a surefire cure. I learned it from an old medicine man, and it works wonders." There was a long pause and then he looked over at Lani.

"Can you please make some water sounds for me?"

Water sounds? I thought. What the heck . . . ?

"Sssssspppppssssshhhhh . . . ," Lani began. "Ssssss-ppppsssssshhhhh . . . ," she went on, imitating a steady stream. "Sssssspppppssss . . ."

Suddenly I got it.

"Oh, no!" I yelled. "No way! You are *not* going to . . ."

But he was going to. The crazy man looming over me was going to pee on me!

"Ahhhh . . . ," Geek said. "We're in business now. Here we go. . . ."

I thrashed around wildly on the table. "No!"

"Hey!" Geek yelled. "Hold him still, Lani!"

"I'm trying!" she shouted back. "I'm trying!"

I kept moving while Geek aimed.

"Sit on him!" Geek yelled.

"What?" she said.

"Come on!" Geek told her. "You have to knock him out or something. I'm running on empty here!"

I was still twisting fiercely, making it hard for Lani to keep me in one position. Finally, she slipped and fell hard on me. "Whooaaaa!" she called. "Cody? Are you okay?"

But I couldn't answer. I'd been knocked out cold again.

With a sigh, Lani looked over at Geek and waited for him to finish.

CHAPTER 9

BACK ON THE NORTH SHORE,

where the contest was going to happen, everyone was still talking about my fight with Tank Evans.

In fact, the reporters from SPEN were discussing my wipeout in great detail on TV.

"The Big Z Memorial Surf-Off hasn't even begun, but we've already lost our first surfer," one reporter announced. The network showed footage of my wipeout again and again so the whole world could see it. "And with just four days until the starting horn sounds, it's anybody's guess as to what this year's contest has in store."

As for Reggie, he was busy doing photo sessions with the other surfers while the moviemakers interviewed him again. This time he wanted to talk about me.

"Let me tell you something about Cory," Reggie started, posing with a penguin who was holding a surfboard plastered with Reggie's picture.

"Cody," a movie guy corrected him. "His name is Cody Maverick."

"Right. Cody. Well, Cody had potential."

Mikey snapped the picture, and Reggie turned back to the filmmakers.

"Sure. He was rough around the edges, but he had that something special. In fact, he reminded me of a young Big Z." He shrugged. "Too bad he couldn't stand up on the board. Big Z could stand up on the board. Next!"

"Rory!" Mikey motioned to a surfer from Australia. "Rory! You're up!"

Rory stepped up and gave Reggie a great big bear hug. "G'day, cobber!" he said to Reggie. "It's fair dinkum to be here," he added.

Do you know what that means?

Me neither!

"Uh . . . I'm just going to need you to smile, Reggie," Mikey reminded him.

Reggie was looking at Rory with a disgusted expression.

Rory, meanwhile, was checking out Reggie's big hair.

"That's a real didgeridoo you got there, mate!" He reached over to touch it.

Reggie quickly backed away. Then he pointed a finger right in the dude's face. "Touch the hair and you'll never surf on those feet again."

As soon as Mikey snapped the picture, Reggie dropped the smile and pushed Rory away. "Next!"

"Do you think you pushed Cody and Tank too far yesterday?" the filmmakers asked him.

"Hey!" Reggie glared at them. "Did I force that kid to go in? Huh? Did I hold a sharp stick to his head?"

Tatsui Kobayashi, a surfer from Japan, approached Reggie next. He was carrying a surfboard wrapped in seaweed.

Reggie made a face."What is this stuff, sushi?"

I mean, the guy has no tact. No tact at all.

"Top secret design," Tatsui said politely. Then he pulled the board away from Reggie. "Must not reveal until competition."

"What? That's not a Reggie board under there?"

Tatsui shook his head. "No."

"Then no picture! Next!" Reggie pushed him away.

"Look, forget Cody," he went on. "If you guys knew what you were doing, you'd be making this movie about me."

43

The next surfer, Juan Carnavale, had scrapes and cuts all over his body.

"What happened to you?" Reggie said. Then he noticed something on Juan's rear end and his eyes went wide. "Hey, Mikey, have you seen this?"

"What . . . ? Oh . . . that . . . ," Mikey answered slowly.

Juan turned around to show what Reggie had noticed—a row of shark teeth stuck in his rear end.

Juan shrugged. "Doesn't hurt, man."

Reggie rubbed his temples, looking exhausted. "This one's another loser . . . ," he murmured. "What I need is another Big Z. I still remember the day I found him. There he was, hanging out with a bunch of beach bums, and I took one look at him and said, 'This kid's got talent and Reggie Belafonte's got the credentials to make him get noticed!'"

Just then Reggie spotted the next surfer in line.

"A chicken!" he exclaimed. "This is getting ridiculous!"

Chicken Joe walked up to him. He was so worried about what had happened to me after the fight with Tank, he didn't even realize that there was a photo session going on.

"Dude," he said to Reggie. "Have you seen my friend, Cody? He's kind of like a penguin. . . ."

Reggie grimaced and leaned back to get away from him.

"Er . . . Maybe you should go find him?"

"Dude! You are so right!" Chicken Joe said. "Thanks, man!"

Mikey quickly clicked a picture. Then Joe took off, calling my name as he headed toward the dense jungle.

"Cody! Where are you, buddy?"

Now that's what I call loyalty.

CHAPTER 10

WHERE I WAS WHEN CHICKEN JOE

started looking for me was sound asleep inside Geek's tree house.

Lani had to go to work. "Okay," she told Geek. "You two have a good day."

"Hey, hey, hey!" Geek leaped out of the hammock and stood in her way. "I don't think so, Lani. What you pack in, you pack out!"

"Geek . . . ," Lani said softly.

"No!" Geek crossed his fins stubbornly.

"Promise me you'll take care of him," Lani said.

Geek groaned. "Aaaahhhh, Lani."

"Geek!" she said sharply. "Promise me!"

"Okay! Okay! I'll take care of him."

Lani frowned at him, still unsure.

"Geez," he grumbled. "As soon as you go, I'll go

46

inside and get him breakfast, okay?"

Lani reached over to hug him. "Thank you. It's good for you to have something to do."

Geek's idea of "getting me breakfast" was to grab a pineapple off a shelf. I was still sound asleep when he chucked it at me, bonking me in the head.

"Ow!" I cried.

He didn't care that he'd just given me another lump on my head. "That was your breakfast. Eat it walking," he commanded. "Come on."

I forced myself up, my whole body still aching from yesterday's accident. I limped along after him through the thick jungle, with no idea where he was taking me. All I could think about was my wipeout. I had blown it. I had ruined my chance to surf in this year's Big Z Memorial Surf-Off.

Ahead of me Geek pushed a low tree branch out of the way. It snapped back and hit me right in the face.

"Ow!"

Geek didn't even notice. "The trail's up here somewhere," he said, gesturing vaguely. "When we get there, you're on your own, kid."

I sighed, still depressed. "Who cares? My life is over anyway."

"Your life's over?" He turned around and stared at me.

"Because of one lousy wipeout?"

"Uh . . . yeah!" I said. Then I shook my head. This guy was an overweight loser. He didn't understand anything.

"You don't know what it's like to want to surf in the Big Z," I blurted out. "Then everything comes down to this one moment, and you screw it up, and you can never get it back.

"I bet *he* never screwed up," I added, thinking of Big Z. I reached up to touch my necklace.

But it was gone.

"Oh, man," I said in a panic. I looked all around the ground near my feet. "I must have lost my necklace somewhere."

"Big deal." Geek blew me off. "You can get yourself another one at one of Reggie's trinket shops."

"It's not just any old necklace," I told him. "He gave it to me himself."

"Who?" asked Geek.

"Big Z. When he came to Shiverpool, my hometown."

Geek look surprised. "He gave it to you personally?"

I nodded. "He believed in me when no one else did. He told me, 'No matter what, find a way. 'Cause that's what winners do.'"

Geek was still staring at me.

"It's just funny, you know," I went on, "what a loser

48

I turned out to be."

Geek kept walking toward the trail. "Who cares what Big Z said—or what I say, for that matter. You've got to do things your own way."

"I don't have a way," I told him. "That's the problem."

By now we'd reached the trail. Geek stood there for a second, lost in his thoughts.

Finally, he pointed toward the trail. "Well, uh, now you have a way," he said. "Just follow this trail. It'll take you back to North Shore."

He turned and began to shuffle off. "Okay. Nice meeting you. Good luck."

I watched him go, and then glanced toward the path. But instead of moving, I dropped down on an old log.

"Where am I supposed to go?" I murmured. "Back to North Shore where all the surfers are hanging out? I can't show my face there."

The filmmakers were watching me.

"What about going home?" one asked.

"Are you kidding?" I shook my head. "My brother, Glen, would be thrilled if I went back now, before the contest even started."

I pictured Glen waiting at home for me, he and his egg hatcher buddies with painted letters on their chests, like those crazy football fans: W . . . E . . . L . . .

49

WELCOME HOME, LOSER.

That's exactly what my brother would say to me.

Suddenly, I couldn't stand the camera watching me anymore.

"Turn it off, guys," I said sharply. "Just turn it off."

CHAPTER 11

I HAVE NO IDEA HOW MUCH TIME

passed while I was sitting on that log, trying to decide what to do next. I wasn't ready to go back to Antarctica. And I definitely couldn't head back to North Shore and face Reggie and the surfers.

I was still sitting there, trying to figure it all out when someone pushed through the brush.

It was Geek.

He looked surprised to see me. "What are you still doing here?"

"I don't know," I told him. "What are you doing here?"

He dropped my Z necklace onto the log.

"Oh, wow!" I grabbed it and put it back around my neck. "Thank you."

"You'd better keep that knot tight," Geek warned me.

"If you lose it during one of your surf contests, it's a goner."

"Don't worry. I'm not going to be in any more surf contests," I reminded him.

"Oh, no?" Geek gave me a look. "There's more to surfing than beating Tank Evans, you know."

I didn't bother to reply. I had come to Pen Gu Island to be part of the contest, and that was that.

Geek scratched his head and stayed silent for a second. Then he noticed the log where I was sitting.

"Hmmm . . . koa . . . ," he murmured.

"Huh?"

"That's koa wood," he explained. "The best surfboards in the world are made from koa."

He knocked on the log a few times. Then he looked back at me. "Do you have a koa board?"

"I don't have a *board* board," I reminded him. "Mine got smashed to pieces on the way here."

"Well, do you want to make one?" he asked me.

"Nah." I shook my head.

Geek peered at me, frowning. "Get off your butt," he said suddenly. "We're going to make a board."

I glared at him. "Geek. I just said—"

He shoved me off the log before I could finish, then

started pushing it from behind.

I stood there, just watching him for a minute. Then I went over to help.

Remember how I told you that Chicken Joe was looking for me?

Well, he had wandered deep into the jungle.

"I know Cody's out here," he murmured. "I can feel it."

The filmmakers caught some of it on tape.

"Aren't you nervous, Chicken Joe?" one asked. "The jungle's pretty dense."

"Dude, the jungle is one of the most peaceful places on the planet. Right now, Mother Nature is trying to give me a hug. And I'm going to let her."

Chicken Joe hugged a tree. "Thanks, Mother Nature. Now I've got to hug it forward, man. Dude, what's your name? Can I give you a hug?"

Chicken Joe hugged the filmmaker. "Love you, man! Now *you* have to hug someone. . . . Here! Hug your cameraman!"

The filmmakers hugged each other.

"So, see, my friends, we are all surrounded by love," Chicken Joe declared happily. "We are all one—"

Thwack!

Everyone froze as a sharp spear suddenly pierced the tree trunk right next to Joe.

"Oh . . . okay," Chicken Joe said, looking at it. "It's cool." Then he ducked under the spear and started looking for me again.

"Cody! Where are you?"

CHAPTER 12

GEEK WAS TRYING TO TIE A VINE

around one end of the koa log so we could tow it out of the jungle.

The film crew chose that moment to ask me some more questions.

"So, Cody. What about the surfing contest?"

"I don't even want to think about that right now. But this Geek guy, he saved my life," I went on, "and now he's going to help me make a surfboard, which is cool."

Geek heard me talking. "What are you doing?" he said, annoyed. "For your information, I could use a little help over here."

"What? Oh . . . uh . . . okay," I said. Then I hurried back over.

As we dragged the log through the jungle, I tried to find out more about Geek.

"What kind of name is Geek?" I asked.

"It's my name," he panted.

I stopped to catch my breath, too. "Okay. So why do you live in the middle of the jungle, making surfboards? I'm just trying to understand."

"Forget the twenty questions, kid," Geek said, annoyed again. "Let's just get the board made, okay?"

"Okay." I shrugged. "I just wanted to know. . . . Are you a surfer? Or do you—"

He answered my question by jerking the log forward as hard as he could.

I lost my grip and fell flat on my face in the mud. "Ooomph!" I spat mud out of my mouth. "Ha, ha. Very funny!"

"Less talk, more pushing, hmmm?" he snapped back.

I stood up and pushed. "Why are we pushing it anyway?" I wanted to know. Why can't we just roll it?"

I rolled the log sideways to show him. "Like this."

"Oww!" Geek yelled. "That was my foot!"

"Oh! Sorry!" I felt terrible. "Sorry, Geek! Is it broken?"

Without thinking, I let go of the log to look at his foot.

"Hey! Hey!" shouted Geek. "The log! It's getting away!"

The two of us took off after it.

"Cody! Cody!" he was yelling at me. "The log!"

"I know! I know!"

The log careened out of control down the steep hillside. Geek managed to get out in front of it and stop it before it started down another steep slope.

"Whew!" He breathed.

But then the log started to slip again.

"Cody! Grab the vine! Grab the vine!" Geek shouted at me.

I tried, but the vine kept slipping from my fins. The log started down the steep hill, with Geek plastered to the front end of it.

"Geek!" I yelled.

"Ahhhhhhhhhh!" He was screaming at the top of the lungs. "Grab the vine!"

Desperately, I ran after the log. But by now it was far, far ahead of me.

And headed straight for the edge of a cliff.

"Ahhhhhhhhh!" I heard Geek yell. "Aahh—" Abruptly, his voice trailed off, and there was a loud *Bam!*

My heart sank. I dashed to the edge of the cliff and peered over.

"Oh, man! Oh, no!" I murmured. There was no sign of Geek below.

Just then a flipper grabbed hold of my leg.

"Aaah!" I cried, startled.

Using my leg, Geek hoisted himself onto solid ground.

He was panting hard as he spat out the words.

"What . . . part . . . of . . . 'Grab . . . the . . . vine' . . . don't . . . you . . . understand?"

"Oh, man!" I was relieved to see him. "I totally thought I had killed you. I'm so glad you're all right."

Geek scowled at me. "Yeah. Thanks for nothing. Next time when I say, 'Don't roll the—"

"Hey!" I cut him off, spotting something in the distance beyond the cliff. "What's that?"

Geek followed my gaze. "It's a beach," he told me. "Sand, water, sun. You seen one, you seen 'em all. C'mon. Let's get out of here."

I shook my head. This wasn't just a beach; it was the most amazing, beautiful stretch of sand and ocean that I had ever seen.

"Come on," I said. "Let's go check it out!"

As I headed toward the cliff, I saw there were some rock steps built into it. Unfortunately, as I headed toward the cliff, I accidentally stepped on Geek's fin.

"Ow!"

He lost his balance and fell behind me. I cringed as he tumbled down each step, one by one.

"Ow! Ach! Ugh! Ow!"

"Sorry, Geek, sorry!" I called.

But by the time we reached the bottom, I'd

forgotten all about his fall.

If heaven has a beach, I thought, gazing around in awe, *it would look like this.* The sea sparkled turquoise in the sun. The sand was a fine white powder, like sugar.

Wow. I drew in a breath.

Nearby, Geek rolled onto the beach still covered in vines and leaves.

"Hey!" I called to him, spotting something cool. "Look, Geek! It's an old, abandoned board shack!"

I hurried over to get a look.

The shack was old and run-down. Inside it was dark, and cobwebs clung to a bunch of surfboards leaning against the walls.

I stepped up to look more closely at the boards.

"Whoa . . . ," I said softly. "I recognize these boards. They belonged to Big Z! This is the one he rode in the Australian Open!" I said. "And this one . . . It's the board he rode when he came to Shiverpool. . . ."

It was amazing.

I turned to look at Geek. "This is Big Z's place, man! This is where he hung out! This is where he made his boards! Did you know this was here? Why didn't you tell me?"

Geek looked as if he were in a trance. He was

walking toward another old shack on the beach. Its roof was caved in, and there was stuff lying around everywhere. Slowly, Geek brushed sand off a sign hanging over the shack. . . .

BIG Z'S PLACE

I watched him pick up a bar of surf wax and sniff it.

"Geek . . . ?" I said softly.

He didn't even know I was there. Still acting dazed, he strummed an old ukulele resting against the wall. Then he gazed around at all the notes and leis tacked up everywhere, an odd look on his face.

Then it hit me. And hit me hard.

Really? You figured it out, too?

That Geek—an out-of-shape, funny-looking, fat penguin—was really my hero, Big Z Topanga.

HEY, DUDE.
I WANT TO TELL YOU
MY STORY!

I MET "BIG Z" TOPANGA
WHEN I WAS JUST A LITTLE PENGUIN.

Z IS FOR ZURFING

© Reggie Belafonte Productions
All Rights Reserved

REGGIE BELAFONTE:
THE MASTERMIND BEHIND THE BIG Z
MEMORIAL SURF-OFF.

A TALENT SCOUT NAMED MIKEY CAME TO FIND ME FOR THE COMPETITION.

BUT THERE WERE **NO WAVES** TO BE FOUND **THAT DAY!**

I'LL BE SURFING AGAINST
TANK "THE SHREDDER" EVANS.

CHICKEN JOE ALMOST BLEW MY COVER IN FRONT OF LANI! NOT COOL, DUDE!

THE LOCALS MAKE CHICKEN JOE FEEL RIGHT AT HOME.

BiG Z GAVE ME tHiS NECKLACE HIMSELF—
it's MY PRiZED POSSESSiON!

BiG Z tAuGHt ME A LOt
ABOut SuRFiNG.

I RACED LANI THROUGH THE LAVA TUBES.

BIG Z CAME TO RESCUE ME IN THE BONEYARDS **JUST IN TIME!**

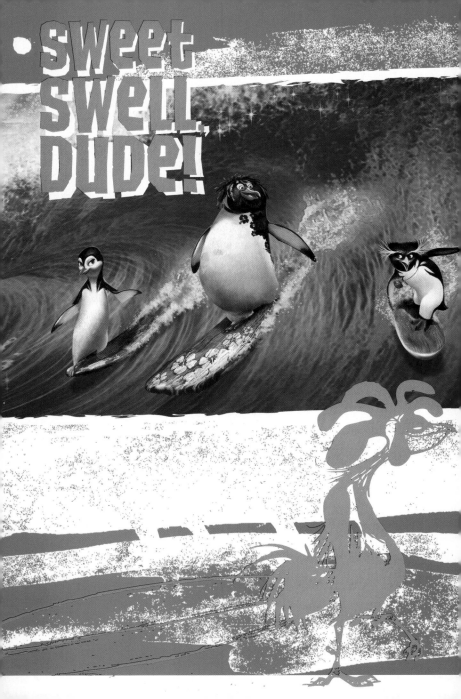

CHAPTER 13

I WATCHED GEEK LOOK AROUND HIS

old shack. I could tell that he needed some space, you know, some time to himself. And I respect that. So I did what any sensitive person would do. I . . .

. . . charged him! Yelling and screaming and exploding with excitement, I raced toward Geek.

"You're Big Z! Ahh-haa! I can't believe it! You're alive! You're alive!"

I hopped around him like a crazy person.

"Why are you alive?" I demanded. "What happened? Tell me! Tell me everything. Start at the beginning and just go! Go!"

"Kid, kid, kid . . . ," Big Z told me. "Relax. You're going to hurt yourself."

But I was way too excited to relax. "And . . . and . . . people said you were dead, but you're not dead;

you're in hiding! Did something happen?" I didn't let him answer. "Something happened!" I guessed. "You saw something you weren't supposed to see! I knew it! That's what happened."

He stared at me. "Are you nuts? It's not a conspiracy, Cody. It's no big deal."

"Oh . . . ," I said, nodding. "Okay. Then tell me what did happen."

He looked away. "I don't want to talk about it."

With that, he stepped inside his old place and shut the door in my face.

"Okay. I got it!" I said to the door. "But I'll be right here if you need anything! You know, if you just feel like talking . . . er . . . whatever." I tried to walk away, I really did. But my feet drew me right back to the shack. "Do you feel like talking now? Do you feel like talking right now?"

His voice boomed from behind the closed door. "Go away."

"Got it. All right. I'm going away. . . . I'm going away." I stepped back toward the shack. "Unless you . . . you . . ."

"Cody!" he yelled at me.

"Okay." I sighed. "Got it."

I sat down on the beach to wait for him, feeling as if it were me who'd just been brought back to life again. I mean, what had just happened was huge. It was going to change everything. Because now I had a plan. And it was to get Big Z—the greatest surfer of all time—to train me so that I could win the Tenth Annual Big Z Memorial Surf-Off.

That was my dream, and I couldn't give up on the dream I'd had for my whole life. Just like the Big Man had told me years ago in Shiverpool, winners find a way, no matter what!

CHAPTER 14

MEANWHILE, BIG Z WASN'T THINKING

about me and my dreams. He was sitting in his old beach shack, remembering who he used to be.

Back in the sixties, he'd hung out on the beach and surfed every day. But after Reggie "discovered" him, things changed—a lot.

One time Reggie made him stand on the sand on a surfboard. A camera framed him against a deep blue sky, making it look like he was really surfing.

"Boy, these sure are some groovy breakers," Z had to say in a stupid fake voice. "I sure would like to ride them with you. So why don't you come to Reggie's big new contest. It's coming up real soon—"

Z stepped off the board and walked toward the camera. "Cut!"

"No! No! Don't cut!" Reggie exclaimed. "Get back

on the board, Z!"

"I'm sick of this. I should . . . I should be out there riding with my buds."

Mikey walked over and fussed with Z's hair.

"I didn't know you had any buds left, Z," Reggie said.

"Are you kidding? I've got loads of—"

"Really?" Reggie gave him a skeptical look. "You think they'd care about you if you weren't the champ?"

Z didn't know what to say to that.

"Now get back on the board and finish the commercial, champ," Reggie said.

Reluctantly, Z obeyed.

"Action!" Reggie called.

Just then, Z snapped back to the present and realized there was another camera watching him.

"Guys?" He poked his head of the surf shack and called to the movie crew. "Can we talk?"

"Sure. Sure."

"Could you guys . . . ?" Big Z started. "Could you cut the last part of the film?" He laughed nervously. "I'm supposed to be dead, and, uhh. . . . I don't think that anyone's really ready for . . ."

"Do you want to talk about it?" one of the guys asked, concerned.

"No." Big Z shook his head. "Just cut that scene,

okay? I don't want it in the movie."

"Okay," they agreed.

While Big Z was talking to the movie guys, I sneaked around and stole one of his surfboards. I picked one of the really long ones he'd used way back when.

I paddled out. When the right wave came, I hopped up onto the board and let out a yell.

Big Z flew out of his shack. "Hey!" he shouted. "What are you doing, Cody? Who said you could take my board?"

I was having too much fun to let him bother me.

"Turn that board around! Get back here!" he yelled.

"Nahh." I grinned at him. "Come out here and show me some moves!"

"No! No! No!"

"Come on, Z. Grab a board and come out!"

"Hey, if you want to kill yourself, go right ahead. It's fine with me. Just don't mess up my board."

I hate to admit it, but I was having a hard time handling the long board. "How do you turn this thing?" I yelled.

"It's not a short board! You have to sit back on it," he told me. "Let—"

Just then a wave smashed over my head.

Big Z scowled. "You mess up my board, Cody, I'm messing up your other foot!"

"Hey. I'm just trying to ride this . . . this canoe . . . or whatever it is!"

"Well, stop trying so hard!" Big Z ordered. "Just relax."

"What do you mean?" I shouted back. "I—" Another wave knocked me down.

"Long, smooth strokes!" Big Z coached me from the shore. "No! Not like that! Dig deep! Dig! Come on!"

"I am! I'm digging!" I surfed down the face of a wave.

"Keep the nose up! Keep it up! Watch it!" Big Z told me. "You're pearling. . . . You're pearling. . . . Aaaahhhh, you're pearling. . . ."

I wiped out on the next few waves. When I glanced toward shore again, Big Z looked mad.

"What are you doing?" he barked.

"Surfing!" I shot back. "You want to come help me, come out here and show me, okay? Because I can't learn anything with you standing out there on the sand."

"Well, then, you're not going to learn anything," he answered me. "Now come on in."

I could be just as stubborn.

"I'm not coming in until you come out!"

"Oh, you're coming in all right!" With that, he turned away from the ocean. "He's not even watching the wave. . . ." he muttered to the filmmaker.

"What wave?" the filmmaker asked.

Big Z pointed to the water without even looking at it. "That one."

Out of nowhere, a wave built behind me. And then, still not looking at the water, Z began to count backward.

"Five . . . four . . . three . . . two . . ."

He found a stick on the beach and drew a large X in the sand.

The wave crashed on top of me.

Next thing I knew, the board and I had washed up on the beach, landing smack-dab on the X Big Z had drawn.

"Wow! That was amazing!" the cameraman said.

Z walked over and picked up his surfboard from me. "Don't touch my stuff, man."

I was coughing up water and gasping for air. "I couldn't help it. I . . . I just wanted to surf with you."

"Yeah, well . . ." He glowered at me. "Too bad because I don't surf anymore."

"What?" I shook the water off myself. "What do you

mean you don't surf anymore?"

"Hey, do you want to learn how to surf the right way?"

I squinted at him. I didn't know. . . . Was he just playing with me, or was he offering to train me?

"Sure," I answered slowly. "I want to learn how to surf the right way."

"Then you've got to make your own board," he told me. "Get up."

I got to my feet and started to follow him.

"But . . . I . . . What do you mean, you don't surf any—"

He held up a fin, cutting me off.

"Can I just ask one question?" I tried again. "About how you—"

The fin went up again.

I sighed, frustrated. I wanted to ask more questions. I couldn't understand it. Big Z had been like the greatest surfer in the world, winning contests, starring in commercials, touring the world. I'd heard the filmmakers interviewing some of Big Z's old friends the other day. They'd said that Big Z had never been afraid of a single wave. And that people—especially girls— had lined up around the block to get his autograph.

So why didn't Big Z want to surf anymore?

I remembered something that Big Z's old friend

Dennis had told the moviemakers.

"I mean, he had it all. Big Z was the biggest success surfing had ever seen. And that's when that Belafonte guy entered the picture. After that, everything went downhill."

Hmmm . . . Dennis had given me something to think about.

CHAPTER 15

Z AND I CARRIED THE KOA LOG TO A clearing near Z's old shack.

"Hold it steady. Got it?" Big Z asked.

I grunted. "Yeah."

Together we lifted it onto two sawhorses.

Big Z found a piece of charcoal. I watched him draw a shape on the top of the log.

This is so cool, I thought. To be here with Big Z, making my own surfboard, was beyond anything I'd ever imagined.

"All right, I drew this pattern as a guide," Big Z told me. "Now do you want to have your board with a lot of rocker or just a little?"

"Uhhh . . . ," I fumbled, not sure what to say. "I guess I like the ones with—"

"What you want is something in between," Z

71

answered for me. "Trust me. I'm the expert here, okay? So here are your shaping tools."

He showed me a bunch of tools but didn't hand any over.

"Now, remember, the board's already inside there somewhere. What you're doing is, you're trying to find it . . . reveal it. . . . Got it?"

Whatever that meant.

"Uh-huh . . ." I nodded.

"Every carve, every cut counts," Big Z went on.

"Okay," I answered. I grinned as I pictured myself standing on top of a brand-new board. This was going to be awesome.

Big Z gave me a look. "Why are you smiling? Don't smile!"

"I'm not smiling," I said quickly. "I'm just, you know, excited."

"This isn't like hacking a piece of ice, Cody!" he said, scowling. "Carving a board takes patience and finesse."

"All right already!" I shot back. "Will you just give me the tools? Please!"

Big Z handed them over.

"Sheesh," I muttered. Then I walked over to the log and started pounding the wood, pretending I knew what to do.

When Z saw me, he practically had a heart attack. "What are you doing?"

He snatched the tools from me.

"Look, if you're going to do this, Cody, do it right! All right, like, first of all . . ." He demonstrated with one of the tools. "You need to go with the grain. . . . With the grain . . . You see what I'm doing here? You let the tool do the work. You see? Just like when you're riding the wave. You let the wave do the work. You don't fight the wave. You can't fight these big waves, Cody."

I nodded, watching him. "Long strokes. Loads of finesse," he went on. "Find the board within the tree. Nice and easy."

"Yeah, I got it," I said. "I think I can take over now."

But Big Z just kept on doing what he was doing, as if he were in some kind of dream state.

"Uh . . . Z . . . ," I tried again. "Maybe I can do it now."

Big Z didn't hear me. He was somewhere else. I leaned in really close to him and spoke right in his ear.

"Can I do it now?"

That did the trick. Big Z woke up and looked at me, an embarrassed expression on his face.

"I got carried away. Sorry about that, kid."

He handed the tools back to me. "It's your board."

"My board," I repeated with a nod. "And I go with the grain. I got it."

"Don't forget to eyeball it once in a while," Big Z reminded me.

"Okay. Long strokes. With the grain," I repeated.

"Well, not too long," he told me.

I picked up the carving tool, suddenly a little nervous. "Here we go. . . ." I touched the tool to the wood, about to make my first cut.

"You're doing it all wrong," Big Z blurted out.

"Aaagh!" I cried in frustration. "Will you just . . . Will you just leave me alone? I can't do it with finesse when you're in my face! Just let me make the board!"

There was a really long pause.

Then Big Z spoke up again. "Do you want my help?"

"Do I want your help?" I echoed. "No, I don't want your help." I spelled it out slowly for him. "I-do-not-want-your-help."

"Oh." Big Z looked at me sadly. "In other words, you don't want my help?"

"Right. I don't want your help."

"Oh . . . ," Big Z sighed.

"Okay?" I tried to get him to understand. "I just want to make my own board."

But I'd obviously hurt his feelings.

74

"Fine! Build the board yourself, man, all right?"

"Thank you," I replied. "I will."

He walked away, muttering stuff under his breath. "I don't care what the board looks like. You're the one who's got to ride it."

"Fine. Thank you," I replied.

He whirled around and marched over again. "The board's in the log somewhere, Cody. . . . You just have to—"

"Fine! Thank you!" I pointed to a spot in the distance. "Walk over there! Please!"

Reluctantly, he walked away again. "Don't cut yourself or anything," he called over his shoulder.

CHAPTER 16

you asked me about chicken joe.

It turns out that while Big Z and I were making my board, Chicken Joe was still wandering through the jungle, where he had bumped into some natives.

Let me put it this way: They weren't exactly the friendly type.

In fact, they had strapped poor Joe to a long pole and were carrying him through the jungle like a piece of meat.

I know. I know. It's definitely not funny. But I can't help laughing a little bit. I mean, Joe actually thought he was getting VIP treatment from these guys!

He told the moviemakers that they were his new friends.

"They treated me like a king. They put me in their royal hot tub and danced all around. They even served me food while I was in there!"

What really happened was the natives were adding vegetables to the "hot tub." They were using Joe to make chicken soup!

"As enjoyable as it was to get special treatment, I still had a vision of my quest," he said into the camera. "I needed to find my buddy. So I got up out of the hot tub and got on my way.

"'Okay, see ya!' I told the natives. And even though I had to go, it felt really good to be wanted."

The natives wanted him all right! They chased after him, yelling and throwing their spears.

As for me, I chipped away at my surfboard. At first Z sat away from me, tuning his ukulele and pretending not to be watching me.

Finally he couldn't take it anymore. He walked over and stood next to the board, shaking his head.

"What?" I demanded.

"Nothing," he said, chuckling.

"Come on," I said. "What?"

"It just reminds me of the first board I made," he said.

At first I thought that was a good thing. "Really?" I said, beaming proudly.

"Really," Big Z said. "What a piece of junk that was!"

"What?" I lost my smile fast. "This is a piece of junk to you?"

Big Z looked at what I'd carved so far. There was wood everywhere, and even I have to admit, the board looked pretty chewed up.

"You think it's good enough for the big waves?" he asked.

"Yeah!" I was defensive. "Of course!"

"Okay. We'll see." Big Z walked off. Three seconds later, he was back, carrying a rock. He put the rock down and started to step onto the board.

"Whoa, whoa, whoa! What are you doing?" I cried.

He looked at me calmly. "Let's just say, I'm a big wave."

"You are a big wave!" I snapped. Before he could climb onto my board, I yanked it off the sawhorses and took off down the beach. Big Z took a few steps after me and then quit.

"Where are you going, Cody?"

"It's *my* board, man!" I called back. "Leave it alone!"

"Why don't you go try it out?" Big Z suggested.

I stopped. "Maybe I will!"

"Good!"

I ran into the water holding the board.

I'm embarrassed to tell you this. . . .

As soon as I landed on it, the board snapped in two. Big Z stood there, rubbing his chin.

I lay on the board for a minute. Finally, I got up and threw the pieces onto the sand. Then I stalked over to Big Z. "I didn't come here to learn carpentry! I came here to surf!"

"What do you think we've been doing?" he replied.

"We haven't been surfing, that's for sure."

"Then you don't know what surfing is."

"Duh. It's about riding waves!" I shot back.

He pointed to the ocean. "Some of my best days out there, I never even caught a wave," he said. He looked away, kicking the pieces of my shattered board.

"I don't even know what that means," I muttered.

"Exactly!" Big Z looked up and pointed to my head. "You know what surfing is about in here." Then he pointed to my heart. "But not in here. You don't know what it's about in here."

I stood there, totally stunned. Where had this come from? What was he talking about? I loved to surf. I always had.

Big Z looked deep into my eyes and then shook his head. "I can't help you."

"What?" I blinked at him.

79

"I can't help you," he repeated. "Sorry." He turned.

I watched him go. Then I stomped off down the beach and ran into the jungle.

I walked for a long time, then finally plopped down on a big rock.

What a jerk, I thought, still furious. Couldn't Z tell that I hadn't finished my board yet? I knew it wasn't ready for the water.

CHAPTER 17

DEEP IN THOUGHT ABOUT MY

conversation with Big Z, I wandered aimlessly through the jungle. All of a sudden I saw Lani! She was holding a bucket and seemed to be looking for something.

"Hey, Lani!" I called out.

"Cody! What are you doing here?" she asked. "You're supposed to be with Geek."

"Yeah . . . well . . ." I scowled. "I had to get away from him. Big Z was driving me insane."

"He's not so bad," Lani said. "I mean, I know he's a little stubborn, but . . ." Her words trailed off and she looked at me closely. "Did you just say, 'Big Z'?"

"Yes!" I told her. "I know all about Big Z, okay? We went down to the beach. . . . I saw the board shack. . . ."

"*The beach?*" Lani echoed. "You got him down to the beach?"

"Well, yeah," I said, confused. "What's the big deal about that?"

Lani shook her head. "I've been trying to get Big Z out of that tree for ten years. I can't believe you got him all the way down to the beach in one day! That is so fantastic!"

I stared at her. "I share your excitement," I said flatly.

She grabbed my face, still excited. "Cody, you don't understand. If Big Z left his house and went down to the beach, he must really think a lot of you."

"Yeah, I bet," I said sarcastically. "You weren't around today. You didn't see the way it happened."

Lani suddenly got an idea. She grabbed me by the fin and tried to drag me away. "You're coming with me."

"Uh-uh." I planted my feet firmly in the sand. "I'm not going anywhere."

"You do *not* want to mess with me," Lani said.

She tugged at me again, goofing around and pretending to box with me. *"Whoa! Ha! Whoa! Ha!"*

I couldn't help myself. I laughed and started to play-box with her.

She swung at me and slipped.

I felt bad. "Whoa . . . Watch yourself!"

She jumped up fast. "I'm fine! I'm cool! Come on, let's go."

This time I didn't argue with her. As we walked along, I asked her questions about Big Z.

"I was a kid when I met him," she told me. "When he wiped out that day, I was hanging out on the beach by myself, and I spotted someone in the water struggling. I jumped in and pulled the guy out and it was Z."

"Wow." I was impressed. "How old were you? Like eight?"

"About that. He's the reason I became a lifeguard," she went on. "But I could never get him to tell me any of the details about his wipeout."

There was a funny look on her face.

"I miss the old Z, though," she said. "He hasn't been the same since he stopped surfing."

We started walking again. Soon we reached a really weird-looking landscape. It was barren and pock-marked with large, dark pits, almost like the moon. White steam curled up from the holes.

"I used to come here with Big Z when we were kids," Lani said softly. "He would carry me up here on his shoulders. It's one of my favorite places on the whole island."

I nodded, looking around nervously. I wasn't sure what she liked about this place. It seemed pretty ominous to me.

Lani was still lost in her memories. "Boy, to be eight years old again . . ."

As I leaned over to look into one of the pits, steam shot up at me. "Okay!" I clapped, suddenly ready to go. "Nice story, Lani, but I'm out of here."

She reached up and pulled two large, thick leaves from a tree. Then she pushed one into my fin.

"What's this?" I asked.

She grinned. "You don't want to get all cut up, do you?" She pushed me toward the edge of a big pit.

"Hey! What are you doing?" I cried.

"Aw, come on, you big baby!"

Another blast of steam erupted from the hole.

"No, no, no . . . ," I protested, trying to back away. "You're crazy. I think I'm better off with Big Z. Please, Lani, just lay off."

I stepped backward into one of the dark pits.

"Aaahhhh!" I screamed as I felt myself start to tumble. "I'm falling!"

CHAPTER 18

LANi JUMPED iNTO THE PiT AFTER ME.

"Whoooo!" she yelled happily.

"Aaaagggh!" I was still screaming.

Somehow I landed on my back on top of the leaf. Lani was sitting upright on her leaf, as if it were a sled.

"Stop fighting it, Cody!" she told me, grinning like crazy. "Just let go!"

I struggled to turn myself around to face forward. We were zipping along, inside some kind of tube.

"Slow down," she called. "It's not a race!"

Slow down? What in the world made her think I had any control over this thing?

Finally, I managed to get myself in an upright position. My leaf slid over a big bump. "Yeoooowwwl!"

Up ahead, we sailed by beautiful waterfalls.

"Isn't this cool?" Lani called.

"Yeah, whatever," I replied. But actually it was pretty cool. I was starting to have fun!

We rocketed around a curve.

"Whoooooo!" Lani called gleefully.

I sailed ahead of her. When we reached a fork, Lani called to me, "Okay, wait! Don't take the left side!"

"Yeah, okay," I called back. But all that mattered to me now was that I had taken the lead.

We flew off the end of the fork. When we landed I was still ahead of her.

"Ha! Ha! Slowpoke!" I teased her.

"Not for long!" she replied.

Our leaves bounced and bumped over some stalagmites. "Huhuhuhuhuhuhuhu. . . ."

I lay on my back for a second. "That's it. I'm so beating you now."

"See you!" Lani said.

Next thing I knew, the path ended—just like that. I flew into the air—and landed in a pool of bubbly green liquid.

Lani skidded to a halt and then climbed off her leaf. She walked toward me.

I jumped up. "Beat ya!"

"Yes, you did," Lani said calmly. She clapped politely.

86

"Congratulations. But if I were you," she went on, "I'd get out of there."

I looked around at the glowing green liquid surrounding me. "Why? This stuff is cool. Look," I added, looking down at my chest, "I'm glowing all over!"

She just laughed and pointed at me.

"It's actually pretty beautiful," I said, tossing some of the green goo in the air. "What is it?"

"See those things?" She pointed up.

I looked up at the ceiling of the tube, where tiny creatures were gathered in clumps.

"They're glowworms," she said.

"Yeah?" I said, still not getting it.

"And you're right below them," she explained patiently.

"You mean . . ." I looked at her in horror.

"Poop!"

"Poop?" I echoed, my mouth dropping open as I looked up again.

That was totally the wrong move. Because—

That's right! That's exactly what happened next.

A drop of poop fell right in—followed by a massive dose of worm poop that covered my whole body.

"Awwww!" Frantically, I spit out the poop and tried to shake the stuff off me.

Lani just sat there laughing. She said later that it was the funniest thing she'd ever seen.

She found me a place to wash off—under a waterfall. I stood under the rushing water, trying to scrub glowworm poop out of my feathers. I was definitely *not* in Antarctica anymore.

Lani sat on a big rock, watching me. "That was pretty cool when we flew around the lava pool and it was right under us, wasn't it?"

I was a little too busy at the moment to make conversation.

"And when we went over that jump?" she added. "Did you see where the steam was coming up in the middle?"

"Uh-huh . . . ," I murmured.

"Did you see any of it?" she asked.

I sighed. "I saw a lot of glowworm poop; that's what I saw."

"Hey, you won the race, right?" She grinned and came closer to me. I mean really close.

"You . . . uh . . . missed a spot," she said softly.

She touched the top of my head and brushed something out of my feathers.

Oh, man.

By now, I was tingling all over. I mean, here I was with this gorgeous penguin standing right next to me.

"Yeah . . . ," I managed to say. "I guess . . . I, uh, rushed the course a little."

She leaned toward me.

"Blaaah!" she burst out. Then she backed away quickly. "Whoo! You still really stink!"

I started washing myself all over again. "Um . . . um . . . ," I stuttered. "I'm probably going to have to catch up with you later, okay?"

"Okay," she agreed.

I was worried she'd get the wrong idea. "You know . . . I'm not, like, ditching you or anything. I just have to . . . uh . . . handle something."

"It's okay. I understand," she said, giving me a nice smile.

She put her fin on mine.

I don't even want to tell you what I did next. The cool thing to do, the right thing, would have been to touch her back. Or kiss her or something. But that's not what I did.

Oh, no. Not me.

I looked at her fin on mine. Then I lifted my fin like I was a karate guy.

"Hi-yah!"

She looked at me.

I backed away fast. It was time for me to get out of there.

"*Bye-yah!*" I said, still using my karate voice.

"*Bye-yah!*" she said back to me.

I headed quickly down the path, hurrying away before I did something else really stupid.

She pointed in the other direction. "It's that way," she said.

I looked at her sheepishly. Then I hurried away to get rid of the rest of the glowworm poop.

CHAPTER 19

WHEN I WAS ALL CLEANED UP,

I went back to Big Z's surf shack on the beach. He was inside, snoring loudly. I tiptoed past, heading for the sawhorses.

I knew exactly what I wanted to do.

I lifted a fresh plank of koa wood and placed it across the sawhorses. Carefully, I drew a pattern on the beautiful koa wood. Then I picked up the tools and under the bright moonlight, I began shaping my new surfboard.

I worked all night long.

When Big Z woke up in the morning and spotted me sound asleep across my new board, he decided to give me a little wake-up call.

Thud!

A heavy pineapple landed in the center of my board.

91

"Whoa! Z!" I startled awake. "Yikes! You scared me!"

But Big Z wasn't looking at me. Instead he was studying on my new board.

Slowly, I sat up.

Big Z walked away and then came back a second later with a stool.

By now I was wide awake. And really, really worried.

"Z . . . No . . . ," I started to say. "Please . . . don't touch it. Not after all my hard work."

He paid no attention to me as he stepped onto the stool and then right onto my board.

"Z, buddy . . . ," I pleaded. "Please don't do it. Please don't do it."

But of course he didn't listen. Instead Big Z stood there on top of my board, giving it his full weight.

"Hmmmm . . . ," he murmured.

Then he jumped up and down on it. Hard.

"Z! I swear, man, if you break it . . ."

But Big Z was still jumping up and down as if my board were a backyard trampoline.

"It's stronger than I thought, Cody!" he said, surprised. "I was sure this thing would snap in two!"

Relief washed over me.

"Thanks, man." I was grinning from ear to ear. "It looks like I finally have a new board."

That night Big Z and I finished working on my board. While I sanded a few rough spots, Big Z worked on the fin. Above us, a white moon lit up the water. It was beautiful.

"Look at that." Big Z gazed out at the glassy waves, an expression on his face that I couldn't read. "They're perfect tonight. That's the best place in the world to be," he went on, "in the tube."

"Really?" I said carefully, not wanting to break his mood.

"Ahhh . . . yeah . . . ," he said dreamily. I could tell he was thinking about the past. "Surfing inside the tube is the best thing in the world—it's better than winning any trophy or traveling around on a promo tour . . . I mean, once you get inside the tube, you never want to get out. . . ."

Another perfect wave broke on the shore. Big Z watched it with half-closed eyes.

"You really miss it," I said softly.

"Mmmm . . . ," Big Z said in that dreamy tone.

I watched his face for a second before I decided to get brave.

"You miss it, Z," I said again. "It doesn't to be over, you know. It doesn't."

He didn't say anything so I kept on talking. "You could still come back. You could surf with the best of them. I know you could!"

He was looking at my board, at the spot that I'd been sanding.

"Watch what you're doing now," he told me.

"Z . . . ," I tried again. "You could do it."

"I had my moment," he said. "And that was a long time ago."

"You still haven't told me why," I prodded him. "Why you . . . You haven't told me anything."

Big Z went back to sanding the fin of my board.

"It's . . . uh . . . a very convoluted answer," he replied. "And guess what? I'm not feeling very convoluted at the moment."

Big Z placed the fin in the back of the board. Together we stood there, side by side, admiring it.

Suddenly, I saw Big Z sniff the air. He sniffed a few more times, and then leaned closer to me.

"Glowworm poop?" he asked.

I sighed. "Gimme a break."

CHAPTER 20

It Didn't take long for the natives to track down Chicken Joe again. In the middle of the jungle, they surrounded him and pointed their spears.

A different guy might have been scared. But not Joe.

"Oh, I get it!" he said. "You guys are hungry! Yeah! That's it. You've got the munchies!"

He reached into his sack and pulled out—

Bingo! You got it!

He pulled out his favorite snack.

"*Squidito on el stickito?*" He offered them some squid on a stick and—they loved it, man!

"Tastes like chicken!" one declared in their own language.

"You guys want some more?" Chicken Joe said. "Not to worry, dudes! I'm loaded."

He took more squid out of his bag and tossed it to them.

Forget about finding me—Joe was too busy now having a party!

The day after Z and I made my board, a perfect swell rolled in—glassy round tubes curling from one end of the beach to the other.

Today is the day, I thought, looking at the ocean. I was finally ready for it.

"Z! Dawn patrol, man!" I shouted, whirling past the shack like a tornado. "Get up!"

I grabbed my board from the sawhorses and dashed toward the water.

"Hey, Z, get a board—it's going off!"

The filmmakers watched me race toward the water. "Is the board all finished?" one asked.

"The board's all ready! Cody's all ready!" I informed them, no doubt in my mind.

They wanted to get a shot of me standing on the beach with my new board. But I wasn't about to stop to pose. "Get in a long shot, boys!" I told them.

Suddenly, someone yanked hard on my board, pulling it right from my fins.

"Huh?" I whirled around.

Z stood there, holding my board. He did not look happy.

"Where are you going?" he demanded.

"I . . . I . . . I thought you said we were going to train. . . ."

"Not in the water!" he said. "Geez, kid, what were you thinking?"

I sighed and let him lead me away from the water. So much for testing my new board.

We spent the whole day training on the beach. First, push-ups.

"Up—down. Up—down. Up—down," Z commanded.

He did them right along with me, but it looked pretty funny. He could barely get his big stomach off the ground.

Next, balancing exercises. I had to balance on my board with a stack of rocks in my fins.

"Unhhhh . . . ," I grunted as Z added more rocks and then still more.

"Hey, hey!" Z snapped. "Watch what you're doing. Pay attention now!"

After that, Z did a "breakdown analysis," explaining the mechanics of a good ride.

"Big . . . you know . . . slow . . . It kinda goes up high, and then, who . . . hoooo . . . and he does a flip and then over the top!"

I had no idea what he was talking about. While he drew complicated diagrams in the sand, I stared off into space.

The last thing we did was learn how to paddle. Only I had to do it not in the water but across the sand.

"Ready? Come on—deep!" he shouted from his cushy spot in a beach chair. "Dig! Dig! Yeah!"

I managed to make my way over to Z.

"Yeah . . . nice," he murmured, sipping a tropical drink.

He made me balance on my board again.

This time he threw water in my face.

"Ha, ha!" He laughed. "Wipeout!"

I leaped off my board and sprinted after him. "You're a million laughs, buddy!"

He ran down the beach.

"Come back here!" I called.

He grinned at me as I caught up. "Easy! Take it easy on me!"

CHAPTER 21

FOR THE NEXT DAY OR SO, WE SPENT
every waking hour on the beach, training.

We slept there, too, resting on our boards in the sand.

One morning I woke up early. The waves were enormous towers of glass stretching up toward the sky. I couldn't take it anymore. All I could think about was surfing—real surfing.

I prodded Z with a fin.

"Come on. Let's go surfing, man! Wake up!"

Z grumbled in his sleep but didn't open his eyes.

"Wakey . . . wakey!" I said in a sing-song voice.

All I got back was a loud snore. *Zzzzzzzzzzzz . . .*

Suddenly, I remembered his idea of a wake-up call. I found a pineapple and threw it at him.

My mouth dropped open when he caught it— his eyes still closed.

"Heh, heh!" He chuckled. "Gotcha!"

Actually, it was time to get him. Before he realized what was going on, I had grabbed hold of his board and pushed it across the sand and right into the water.

Z sat up on his board. "Trying to pull a fast one on me, huh?"

I nodded. "I want to go surfing."

"You've got to get up earlier in the morning for that, Cody," Big Z told me. "That's something that will come with experience. You'll see that . . ."

I stood there on the sand only half-listening to him. As he went on and on about how I needed more experience, how the waves were best at dawn, blah, blah, blah, he had no clue that a huge wave was swelling up behind him.

I bent down to draw in the sand. Then I started counting out loud: "Five . . . four . . . three . . . two . . . one . . ."

At that precise moment, the wave crashed over Z's head. When he washed up on the beach on his stomach a minute later, he lifted himself up—and saw what I'd drawn.

A big fat X.

I stood there grinning at him.

And guess what?

He smiled back at me. The big guy was actually proud. I had finally learned something from him.

Z started to get up. But the waves rushing in knocked him right back down on his butt.

He sat there, water dripping off his feathers, looking at the whitewater all around him.

Uh-oh, I thought, here comes the part where he freaks out on me.

"Are you all right?" I asked.

He didn't reply. What he did instead completely amazed me: He splashed around in the water like a crazy person.

"Z . . . Are you okay?"

He grabbed his surfboard and dashed out toward where more waves were forming.

"Hey! You coming or what?" he called back to me.

For a second, I was too surprised to move or speak. But then I grabbed my board and raced after him.

"Yeah! I'm coming!" I shouted.

And let me tell you, it was awesome. When Z rode in on that first giant wave, he looked as smooth and relaxed as the Big Z I remembered watching years ago. It was like he'd never stopped surfing.

He paddled back out, and we both got into the lineup.

Another wave rolled in.

"This one is yours, Cody!"

I took off. But my timing wasn't right and I wound up oversteering.

He appeared on the wave next to me.

"Relax! Long smooth strokes! Go with the grain . . . ," he coached me, "just like when you were making the board."

I stopped trying to steer my board. This time I let it flow naturally into the groove of the wave.

"There you go! There you go! That's it!" Big Z shouted excitedly.

"Yeah!" I cried. "Whoo . . . hooo!"

We surfed side by side all morning long.

I dropped in on another wave. Behind me the tube was starting to form. I tried to slow down, to get inside.

Z watched me.

"Don't try so hard, Cody! Just—"

It was too late. I wiped out. When I came up for air, I could hear Z still giving me instructions.

"Let it come to you!"

I nodded. "Got it!"

We were still surfing when Lani showed up. She stopped in her tracks when she saw Big Z. "You're in the water!"

He grinned at her. "Yeah! Come on out! Get wet!"

"Come on!" I chimed in.

Lani grabbed a board and paddled out, her eyes still locked on the sight of Big Z on a surfboard.

"This is unbelievable!" she exclaimed. "I am so happy!"

I watched Lani get into position. Right before a wave began to break, she sprint-paddled and launched herself into it.

"I didn't know you could surf!" I called after she'd rode it in perfectly.

She grinned slyly. "You never asked."

Big Z sat in the lineup with Lani by his side. He pointed to a big wave.

"Hey, Code!" he called to me. "Wave of the day!"

I turned to check it out. Sure enough, there was a giant rolling in.

I know what you're wondering. . . . Could I handle it?

You bet I could!

I took a deep breath and began paddling.

A second later, I was riding down the wave's steep face, totally in the groove.

Relax, I told myself, remembering Big Z's words. *Go with the grain.*

The tube was forming. I glanced at it, trying to decide

what to do. Finally, I let it go and finished my ride.

"That's okay!" Big Z said. "There's always another one!"

"Great ride!" Lani added.

Just then another wave rolled toward us. Lani and I watched Big Z drop in.

Whoa . . . , I thought, watching the tube swallow him up. Big Z hadn't surfed in a long time. . . . Was he going to make it out?

I held my breath. And soon, he emerged from the tube, looking completely cool. Lani and I laughed as he turned and bowed to the wave.

We were stoked.

"Big Z is back!" I declared.

Z confirmed that by doing a flip with his board and jumping over the back of the wave.

CHAPTER 22

THAT DAY THE THREE OF US SURFED

till the sun set. And let me tell you, watching Big Z do his thing with the waves was awesome!

While we were hanging out, just having fun, the surfers back at the beach were getting ready for the surf-off. There was just one day left until the contest, and the moviemakers were interviewing each of the surfers.

"What do you do the night before a contest like this?" they wanted to know.

Rory, the Australian surfer, answered first. "I just like to sit around with my mates and talk about how great it's going to be. And trust me, it's going to be great!"

Tatsui sat in front of his board—it was still wrapped in seaweed—with a single candle burning at his side.

"I meditate most of the night. It purifies the mind

and spirit and prepares me for the challenge ahead."

Juan was parked under a coconut tree. "I'm just trying to keep from getting injured before tomor—"

Just then a coconut fell from the tree. Juan managed to dart out of the way just in time.

"I'm okay," he told everyone as another coconut narrowly missed him.

And you probably already know what Tank Evans was doing that night—throwing Tank's Tenth Annual Victory Party.

He sat at the shark bar opening clams while he spoke to the camera.

"Every year I like to throw myself a little victory party."

"But the contest hasn't even started yet," a filmmaker pointed out.

"Yeah, I know." Tank waved away that fact. "But trust me, it's in the bag."

With that, he smashed two clams on his forehead. "Oh yeah!"

I see you rolling your eyes. I know. Tank is a moron.

Next, the camera focused on someone standing alone, looking out at the shrine for Big Z. It was lit by flickering torches.

"What are you doing, Reggie?" asked a filmmaker.

"Every year I come out here and have a moment

of silence for him," Reggie said, looking all serious. "I never told anyone that before. You're the first."

The camera lingered on his face for a moment.

Then Reggie looked over at the camera again. "You get the shot?" he wanted to know.

The cameraman nodded.

Mikey came over. "It was ten years ago," Reggie said. "Ten years ago that we lost Z. Can you believe that, Mikey?"

"No." Mikey shook his head. "I can't."

"Ten years ago tomorrow. Now that was quite a contest," Reggie went on.

"Sure was," Mikey agreed.

"See where you're sitting right now, Mikey? That's where Z was ten years ago tonight."

The movie guys wanted to know more.

Reggie told them about how Big Z had sat in the spotlight while Reggie introduced him to the crowd.

"And tomorrow . . . I know you're all looking forward to seeing your favorite and mine—Zeke 'Big Z' Topanga!"

Z had raised a fin while the crowd applauded. "Thanks . . . Thank you . . . ," he murmured shyly.

"Oh . . . and, uh, there's one more thing." Reggie had looked above the stage. "Mikey."

The spotlight had suddenly moved away from Z to a curtain. Big Z had looked around, a little nervous. He'd had no clue what was about to happen.

Reggie had still been working the crowd. "Now this guy you're about to meet, when I saw him surf, he, well, he made my hair stand on end! Heh, heh . . . Because he's electrifying!"

There was a drum roll.

"And tomorrow you're going to see him take on Big Z," Reggie had gone on. "Now please say hello to Tank Evans!"

Tank had stepped into the spotlight, jumping and prancing around like a champion boxer. The crowd had clapped and jumped to its feet.

"Thank you!" Tank had said, waving. He had gestured toward Big Z. "Let me tell you, it's an honor—a true honor—to be riding with this old man tomorrow!"

Z had shuffled uncomfortably in his seat.

The music had started up loudly again. While Tank had stomped all over the stage, inciting the crowd, Z had climbed slowly to his feet. He had pulled Reggie over to a dark corner.

"What are you doing?" he'd demanded.

"It's called a competition," Reggie had said calmly. "What are you worried about? Losing?"

"Hey—look who you're talking to," Z had shot back. "A champ."

"Then be the champ!" Reggie had started to walk away. Then he'd turned to look at Z again.

"Otherwise, you're nothing."

Z had stared at him for a minute, shaken and confused.

Otherwise, you're nothing.

Tank had still been pumping up the crowd. Then Reggie had stepped in front of the microphone again.

"Thank you, Tank. Hey, everybody! I can't wait for you to see this guy ride. He's doing some fabulous new moves. He's the next generation of surfers."

Z had hung his head. And when he'd slipped away a minute later, no one had seen him go.

CHAPTER 23

THE NIGHT BEFORE THE BIG Z

Memorial Surf-Off, Lani, Z, and I sat around a campfire. While Lani grilled shrimp, I sanded my board and Z strummed his ukulele.

"It's impossible to be down when you're playing a uuuuu-kkkkk-eeeee," he sang in a goofy voice.

Lani and I laughed and applauded for him.

"Uh, Z?" I couldn't resist giving him a hard time.

"Yeah?"

"Is that the only song you know?"

"Yeah, just about," he answered. "Want to hear it again?"

"No!" Lani and I said at once.

We looked at each other and smiled.

"You were awesome out there today," I told her.

She grinned at me. "You weren't so bad yourself."

I pointed to Z. "Thanks to this guy."

He shrugged modestly. "Oh, I just pointed you in a direction." He smiled at me and went back to strumming his uke.

I smiled back, but there was something I wanted to ask him.

"Hey, Z?"

"Hey, what?" he replied. "Did you change your mind about the song?"

He began singing again. "*I used to play this ukulele . . .*"

"No, no . . . ," I hesitated. "I was wondering . . . What I wanted to know was . . ." Finally, I blurted it out. "Will you watch me ride tomorrow?"

". . . *when I has half your age . . .* ," he sang. Then he answered me. "Yeah, we'll both ride, man." He went back to the song. ". . . *in the good old days . . .*"

"No." I shook my head. "I meant, will you come to watch me ride in the *contest* tomorrow?"

He squinted at me in the firelight. "What contest?"

"The Big Z! The one they named after you!" I reminded him. "Remember?"

He sighed. "Yeah, I remember."

"I know it's asking a lot," I added quickly, "but it would mean everything to me if you'd come."

Z didn't reply. Instead he put down his ukulele and stood up, keeping his back to me and Lani. Then he tossed another log onto the fire, sending up a shower of sparks.

"You really want to be a part of all that?" he asked quietly.

"Absolutely!" I replied.

"What do you want me there for anyway?"

"To watch me surf," I told him.

"I can watch you surf right here," he said.

"But the contest isn't here," I reminded him.

He stayed quiet, out of excuses. Then he looked over at me again. "What makes you think you can win, Cody?"

I blinked at him. "Because I'm good! I can do this."

"You really think that a couple of lessons from me is going to make a difference?"

"Yeah," I said. "I do."

He shook his head. "You can't beat Tank Evans, Cody."

"Yeah, I can!"

Z stared into the fire, thinking about something for a few minutes. Both Lani and I watched him, waiting for him to say more.

"You can't beat Tank," he repeated. "You're going to

go out there tomorrow . . . and . . ." He wasn't looking at me. ". . . and you're going to be cocky. You're going to be so sure you can beat Tank that there's not a doubt in your head."

I swallowed. I couldn't see his face, but I was sure he was remembering the last time he'd surfed with Tank Evans. I'd seen the footage on TV so many times, I could picture it perfectly.

Z and Tank had paddled out. By now Z was older and he'd started to get pretty out of shape. All day long Tank had outsurfed Z, performing all kinds of amazing tricks and stunts that had dazzled the crowd.

Meanwhile, poor Z had fallen again and again.

After one more humiliating wipeout, Z had come up to the surface and looked back toward the beach. His fans had been watching him in silence, knowing they were watching the fall of a champion.

I could still see that last terrible scene: Z had turned around and paddled out into a monster wave, and then disappeared behind the spray coming off the top. But this time, I could see something that I'd never quite caught before: Z pushing his empty board into the wave and then dropping back into the water without it.

Moments later, Z's broken board had washed up on shore. On the beach there had been total chaos, lifeguards rushing into the water to find him, women sobbing, Reggie announcing that surfing had lost one of its heroes.

Z looked up at me now.

"That feeling of losing . . . It's the worst feeling in the world. You'll do anything to avoid it.

"Even if it means . . ." He poked the fire with a stick, and then tossed it in to let it burn. ". . . throwing your life away."

I stared at him, thinking as details snapped together in my mind like pieces from a jigsaw puzzle. Z had done it himself. . . . He'd deliberately pushed the board into the wave. . . .

"That's why you dropped out," I said suddenly.

Z didn't reply. Instead he just stared at the sand under his feet.

I was shaking my head over and over. I couldn't stop myself. "No . . . no . . . no . . . no . . . How could you?"

Z sighed. "Give it a rest, Cody."

"I thought you were the one guy—"

"We all make choices," Z cut in. "That was mine."

It sure as heck wasn't going to be *my* choice.

"Well, that's you, man," I snapped. "Not me. I can beat Tank Evans." I turned to Lani, who'd been sitting there very quietly this whole time. "Lani. You know I can do this."

She dropped her head. "I don't want to have to pull you out again, Cody," she said softly. "You're just not ready."

"You're not good enough," Z chimed in. Then he repeated the words. "You're not good enough."

I stood. "Who are you to talk, Z? You had it all. I've never had anything! I've never had anyone look up to me or care about me like people cared about you. And what did you do? You threw it all away!"

I fought back tears.

"I'm going to do this tomorrow," I told them both. "And I'm not going to lose. Because if I ever end up like you, Z . . ."

I didn't finish the thought, but Z got the message. He stood up, an angry look on his face. Without saying a word, he stalked off, disappearing into the dark jungle.

Lani hopped to her feet. "Z! Z!" She took off after him, leaving me there alone.

I reached for the necklace hanging from my neck, the one I'd worn ever since I was a little kid and Big Z had come to Antarctica. Everything I'd been living for since then was wrapped up in this little shell.

"You meant more to me when you were dead," I said bitterly. Then I yanked it off my neck and threw it into the sea.

CHAPTER 24

MORNING FOG HUNG LOW OVER THE
jungle as I made my way along the path, my new surfboard tucked firmly under one fin. As I drew closer to the
beach, I could hear a megaphone blaring. My stomach
churned like whitewater.

You can do this, I told myself. *It doesn't matter what
anyone else says. You can beat Tank Evans.*

I stepped onto the beach and then stopped to take
in the scene. Hundreds of spectators lined the sand.
Vendors walked up and down the beach carrying
different kinds of food and surfing trinkets. Brightly
colored banners flapped in the breeze. Above them all
was the one with the SPEN logo—Sports Penguin
Entertainment News.

Mikey was making announcements over the PA
system.

"And we want to give a special thanks to our friends at SPEN for providing coverage today."

On the sand surfers waxed their boards. Kids sat high up on parents' shoulders, taking in the spectacle, too.

I glanced at the ocean. Dark waves crashed along the shoreline. And above the water, the sky looked gray and ominous.

I swallowed hard and forced myself to keep going. As I walked along the sand, almost nobody noticed me. Except for the few people who pointed.

"That's the kid who wiped out," I heard someone murmur. "I can't believe he's back. . . ."

Behind me a familiar voice rang out. "Cody!"

Chicken Joe ran over and gave me a big hug. "I found you!"

"Yeah, I'm here," I said, trying to sound cool. "Good to see you, Joe."

"I've been looking all over for you, buddy!" he told me. "You've got no idea!"

"Here." Reggie kept shoving forms in my direction. "Sign there and there. Also this . . . You don't have to read it. . . . It's standard stuff. Oh, and this one, too."

While I signed Reggie's forms away, Chicken Joe kept hugging me.

"Okay, Joe, that's enough," I said finally. "I'll see you out there, right?"

He looked excited. "This is going to be fun, huh? Okay, well, I'll see you in the lineup."

As I walked away from the registration table, Reggie picked up a horn.

"Folks! This is very exciting! Cody . . . er . . . Maverick, the wipeout king, is back!"

Oh, great. Just what I needed to hear.

"So keep those eyes peeled for some spectacular carnage!" Reggie went on.

All around the beach, people turned to look at me. I clutched my surfboard, wishing I could disappear into the sand.

Someone started laughing loudly.

Tank Evans stood there watching me, a slimy grin on his face.

Stay cool, Cody. I kept going toward the water. *Don't even think about him.*

On the beach, the other surfers were talking and joking around with each other. I dropped my board near them and started waxing it.

"Hey." Suddenly, Lani was there.

"What?" I didn't bother to look up. "Are you here to

tell me that the waves are too big or that I'm not good enough?"

"No . . . I . . ." She sounded flustered. "I just . . . Good luck, Cody," she said finally.

When she walked away, I looked up for maybe a second. Then I went right back to waxing my board.

CHAPTER 25

"SUPFErS READY!" REGGIE'S VOICE
came over the PA.

We were all lined up at the edge of the water,
boards in hand.

A horn sounded, and everyone took off. We paddled
out toward the waves in a big mass.

A large wave formed way out. I paddled furiously to
reach it, and then I sailed straight up its face.

Reggie was calling the action for the fans. "Our
twenty-four surfers are . . ."

The wave broke suddenly, knocking back six of
the surfers.

"Make that eighteen!" Reggie called out, "Our
eighteen surfers are off!"

Tank Evans and two other surfers took the first
wave of the day.

I hate to tell you this, but Tank rode it perfectly. You could see in an instant why the guy had been a nine-time champ.

On the shore the crowd cheered for him.

I waited in the lineup, taking deep breaths to try to keep myself calm. It didn't help that the film crew kept a camera on me the whole time.

Next up were Chicken Joe and two other surfers.

Even though I was really nervous, I enjoyed watching Chicken Joe on his board. He had a funny style— hanging onto the board's rails with his feet—but he hung on and rode like a real pro!

Reggie was amazed by him, too.

"What's a chicken doing here?" he said to the crowd. Then he added, "Who cares? He's incredible!"

Everybody cheered loudly as Joe rode up onto shore. Including the natives who'd been chasing him all over the island. Right now they were chanting his name and gobbling up squid on a stick.

And then it was my turn.

"Here's what you've been waiting for!" Reggie announced. "Give it up for the Wipeout Kid—Cody Maverick!"

The crowd applauded.

I watched a wave build, trying to tune out the scary

fact that it was huge—much bigger than any of the ones I'd been riding on Z's beach.

From her lifeguard station, Lani watched, too. As the wave grew larger, she got more and more nervous for me.

The wave came closer. *It's now or never*, I told myself. *Do or die.* I turned and began to paddle, joining the other two surfers headed for the wave. My heart pounded, and my breathing was hard.

Under my board, the surf swelled, lifting me up. I got to my feet, shaky at first. But then I found my balance—and rode it in!

On the beach, people looked stunned. Lani let out a big sigh.

"What was that?" Reggie said in disbelief.

Then the crowd began cheering for me. "Co-dee! Co-dee!"

Chicken Joe and his buddies did the wave.

"I'll tell you what that was!" Reggie changed his tune. "Incredible!" He chuckled. "You know me, people! Reggie Belafonte loves to keep you guessing!"

CHAPTER 26

RIDING THAT FIRST WAVE SO PERFECTLY

gave me all the confidence I needed. For the next few hours, the "Wipeout Kid" rode wave after wave, still standing tall even after most of the other surfers had been knocked out of the contest.

I was riding down a wave with a face as massive as a football field when I realized that Tank was on my back. I tried to get away.

Up ahead dark shapes loomed under the water. A new wave was building, and as it sucked water into itself, the shapes started to grow clearer. They were sharp points of rock.

Uh-oh, I thought, fighting back my panic. Tank and I were in the Boneyard—the most dangerous place to surf on all of Pen Gu Island.

On the beach, the crowd murmured and moved

closer to watch. Lani, who'd been giving first aid to a surfer, looked up nervously. And of course Reggie was watching, too. That dude had a big grin on his face because he'd just realized that his contest was about to get a lot more interesting!

Below me the water level dropped some more. Razor-sharp rocks rose all around, towering above my head. Frantically, I tried to steer my board to the right, to get around the rocks. But Tank was right there next to me, stopping me from going anywhere but straight ahead into the jagged rocks.

Oh, man.

"Cut it out, Tank!" I shouted.

He let out a low chuckle. No way was he moving.

The muscles in my legs were so tired, they began to shake. Panic washed over me. I was about to fall off my board.

Back on shore, Lani was talking softly to me.

"Don't fight it, Cody. Relax . . ."

I had no choice. Unless I did something different, I was doomed. So I began to let go. And as I relaxed, my board settled, and suddenly I could steer around the sharp rocks.

Tank slalomed around the rocks behind me.

Bam!

He slammed his board into mine.

Relax, I told myself again. I let my board absorb the hit instead of fighting it. It flung me up the slope of a rock. I flew into the air several feet and then landed solidly back in the water.

Whoa! I looked back, amazed at my own smooth trick.

The fans on the beach cheered wildly. They were loving it!

Suddenly, Tank appeared from behind a big rock, his eyes blazing with anger. He shot toward me, slamming into my board. I went flying toward an enormous corkscrew-shaped boulder.

I'm a goner, I thought. *This is it.*

But somehow I managed to relax my body in the nick of time. When I smacked into the rock, I let the water take me.

And it did, spiraling me through the corkscrew and out the other side.

My eyes were shut tight. When I finally peeled them open, I couldn't believe it—I was still in one piece.

Suddenly a loud grinding sound filled the air. Under my board, the water was very shallow—so shallow the reef was scraping the bottom of my board. And looming over me, totally blocking the sky, was another huge wave.

Desperately, I looked around. The rocks surrounding

me were like two times my height. And believe it or not, Tank Evans was coming at me again.

The guy was determined to bring me down.

I looked around. There was nothing in front of me but a wall of jagged rocks. I was trapped.

The wave towered over us. As Tank moved in, the grinding sound grew louder. And louder. When I looked at his board, I saw splinters start to fly. Rocks ripped through his board, shredding it to bits.

Then everything seemed to happen at once.

I braced myself as I reached the wall of rocks. Spotting one shaped like a sickle, I headed toward it. A second later, the wave hit. Tank flew off his board and into the churning water. The wave smacked me hard from behind, sending me right up the sickle-shaped rock. I flew straight up the wave just as it crashed into the wall.

On the beach, everyone was holding their breath.

I hung in the air above the wave for about a split second. And then I dropped into the white foam below.

CHAPTER 27

MY EMPTY BOARD BOBBED ON TOP

of the white water. Lani was already in the ocean, swimming hard toward the spot where I'd plunged in. Chicken Joe had just finished another perfect ride. Now, like everyone else, he stood on the beach completely still, his eyes scanning the water for both me and Tank.

Lani swam hard toward the Boneyards. Suddenly, Tank popped up, out cold.

For a second, she wasn't sure what to do. She looked around for me one last time and then she did what she had to do. She stroked quickly toward Tank.

Meanwhile, I was flailing about, desperately trying to keep my head above water. But every time I got to the surface, the water sucked me back in again. Finally, I managed to grab hold of a rock.

Foamy water swirled all around me. I coughed up

water, completely exhausted. Then I lost my grip on the rock and went under again. The water tossed me all around. I was so tired, I wasn't sure I could fight my way back to the surface this time.

I glanced up. Through the rippled surface above, I spotted something familiar. It was a board—Big Z's board from the shrine, I realized. The sun beamed through the cracks in the surfboard, lighting up the Z carved in its surface.

And then I saw something more amazing on the reef: A figure poked out from behind the board— a large, familiar guy with dreadlocks.

I must be dreaming, I thought. *Is that really . . . ?*

I surged to the surface. There, sure enough, was Big Z.

I coughed up more water. "What are you doing here?"

"You keep losing this darn thing!" he said.

He held up my Z necklace—the one I'd tossed in the water last night when he'd made me so mad.

We both grinned a little. Then Z gestured for me to swim toward him. I started to paddle. But the water was still swirling. I couldn't move forward at all.

"I can't!" I called. "I—" Just then I felt the water sucking me back. Z looked past me, and when I turned, too, I could see a wave.

I'm not lying, dude.

This was the biggest wave I had ever seen in my life. It was growing—and I mean fast—along the horizon.

Po Chu, I thought nervously. This massive wave must be the one that Pen Gu natives called Po Chu, the crusher.

Z watched it, too. "Dig!" he urged me. "Cody, dig faster!"

Obediently, I paddled faster. Z leaned off the rock as far as he could, holding out his fin for me to grab. White water splashed dangerously around him. We both knew that if he fell in, he was a goner.

I kept paddling. But the water kept sweeping me back. Finally, I grabbed a rock and held fast.

The wave grew bigger. Thirty-five . . . then forty . . . forty-five. . . . Suddenly, the water level dropped.

This was definitely not a good situation.

I clung to the rock.

Then Z's eyes went wide. "Cody!" he yelled. "When I say let go, do it!"

"What?" I shook my head furiously. This rock was my lifeline. There was no way I was letting go.

"Trust me! Just let go!" Big Z said. "You're going to come right to me!" With his fin, he made a great big X over his heart.

Let go? I stared at him. I mean, I was terrified. Did he

really believe that the waves would take me right to him?

But I had no other options. With Po Chu about to crush me, my other choice was to trust Big Z.

He'd already started to count down. " . . . 5 . . . 4 . . ."

In my head I counted, too. " . . . 3 . . . 2 . . ."

I let go. Instantly, the water sucked me back and then right up the face of the wave. On the rock, Z stood and backed up near the shrine board. The water roared all around us.

The wave came fast at Z, with me still near the top of it. Then it slammed down, rocketing me into space.

Z reached out his fins. And it was totally amazing— I landed right there. Right in the big guy's arms.

He grabbed me and ducked behind the shrine board just as the wave crashed into it.

Water exploded all around us. For maybe a minute the board held, protecting us. But then the wave knocked down the board and pulled Z and me back into the churning water.

CHAPTER 28

FROM THE BEACH, THE BONEYARDS

were a froth of white water and fog. When Lani came ashore with Tank, Chicken Joe ran over.

"Where's Cody?" he wanted to know.

When she didn't reply, Chicken Joe and a few other surfers lowered their heads.

You got it. They were thinking the worst.

A few minutes later, my empty board washed up on shore.

"Don't touch that!" Reggie shouted as a surfer went to grab it. He ran over and stood in front of my board, protecting it from the crowd. "This board is a reminder of the young surfer who gave his life for the sport he loved. Cary—"

"Cody," Mikey corrected him.

"Jody," Reggie went on.

"Cody!" Mikey said again. "Cody Maverick."

Reggie closed his eyes reverently. "Young Joey Massingale."

Foam and white water surged all around me and Big Z. When my head finally broke the surface again, I spotted the shrine board nearby. I swam over and pulled myself on top. Then I scanned the water for Z.

Let me tell you, after what we'd been through, I wasn't very optimistic.

"Come on, Z," I murmured. "Don't be dead again. . . . Please don't be dead."

The water churned all around me. The air was cold and misty, and the fog made it hard to see.

Then suddenly I spotted something in the water. Z shot up, sputtering.

"Oh . . ." He gasped for air. "There you are!"

He swam over, and I managed to help him onto the board. We sat there for a few minutes, each trying to catch our breath. We were both totally exhausted.

Z coughed. "I was looking all over for you."

"Me, too," I murmured. Then I glanced through the fog at the shore, where I could barely see the crowd gathered there.

"What now?" I asked.

He shrugged. "I don't know."

"I guess I lost the contest," I said.

Z looked back at me and nodded. Then he said, "Let's go, loser."

He started to paddle. I sat there for a second, surprised. Z was headed toward the beach, where everyone would find out the truth about him.

"Hey!" He turned around and gave me a look. "Want to help me out here?"

I did, and we started our ride out of the Boneyards. As we got closer to the shore, Reggie's voice rose from the fog. And when I heard what he was saying, I started to laugh. I couldn't help it.

"Let's all remember young Joey MacEnroe. He was a new beacon for a new generation. May he rest in peace. Forever." With that, he lowered his head and closed his eyes. The crowd joined him. And then . . .

It was the best.

Z and I climbed off the board and sneaked up behind Reggie.

"So, people . . ." He gestured to my surfboard, propped up beside him. "You can see that this is a pretty special board. Koa wood and everything. Do I hear any bids?" He waited a second. "Do I hear

134

thirty?" The crowd, who'd already spotted Big Z and me, didn't say a word.

"Twenty-nine?" Reggie blared. "Do I hear twenty—"

Big Z chose that moment to lean over and grab Reggie's big hair. "Don't touch his stuff, man," Z growled into his ear.

"Not the hair!" Reggie screamed as Z lifted him off the ground. "Not the hair!"

But it was too late. The hair had ripped right off his head.

"Eewwww!" Big Z was totally grossed out. He flung the mop of hair onto the ground. Reggie scrambled desperately to get it back onto his head.

Mikey stared at it. "I knew it! I knew that thing wasn't real!"

Believe it or not, Reggie still hadn't seen Big Z and me. "Who did this?" he shouted, frantically trying to arrange his hairpiece again. "Who is the stupid—"

Finally, he looked up. When he saw Z standing there, he gasped.

"Z! It's you!"

"Is that Z?" people murmured. "Is that really Big Z Topanga?"

Reggie stared at him in shock. "Where have you

been all these years?"

And then, of course, being Reggie, he quickly remembered the crowd.

"Check it out, ladies and gentlemen! Back from the dead, the now living legend . . ."

"I'm not a legend, man," Big Z cut in. He grabbed the shrine board from me and smashed it on the ground.

There was a long silence. Everyone stared at him, waiting to see what he would do next.

"I was a coward," Big Z said. "When I wiped out that day, I couldn't face you all. So I disappeared. And I don't blame you if you don't want me back."

"Z . . ." His old friend Doris was in the crowd. "It's okay, honey." She hurried forward along with some of Z's other friends. They gathered around and hugged him.

"You're back!" someone said.

Z smiled at his old friends. Then he glanced over at me. "I'm back because of this kid." He put a fin around me.

The crowd cheered. Lani ran over to give us both a big hug.

"Hey, guys!" she said. "You should see the swell on the South Shore!"

"Woooo-hoooo!" Z called. "Who's coming with us?"

I was, that was for sure.

But Reggie was already making new plans for Z.

"This is so terrific," he gushed. "The things we can do together. . . . A Z–Tank rematch! The Big Z Senior Surf-Off. . . . Wouldn't that be great, Z?"

Z glared at him. "Keep your contests to yourself, man! I'm done with all that."

As we started up the beach, everyone followed, leaving Reggie standing there by himself.

"Hey! Come back here!" he shouted. "No one walks away from Reggie! Hey!"

Chicken Joe was at the back of the crowd, surrounded by his buddies—and a group of fuzzball baby penguins. They'd seen him surf and become his number-one fans.

Reggie picked up the huge surfing trophy and forced it into Chicken Joe's arms.

"Joe baby . . . You're the winner, pal, and we need to talk."

"Oh . . . thanks, man," Chicken Joe said, barely paying attention. He pushed the trophy at the kids and looked around for me. "Cody! Wait up, dude!"

"Okay, fine!" Reggie scowled. "Go. See if I care, you worthless pile of miscreants! Who needs you anyway? I'm the one who put Pen Gu on the map. I'm the one who discovered Big Z. I'm the one who put this competition together. *Me!*"

Mikey skittered up to Reggie, holding a long, thin rope.

"Mikey!" exclaimed Reggie. "Where have you been? Come on. This place is a disaster. You've got work to do."

At that, Mikey tugged lightly on the end of the rope in his hand.

It was beautiful. All the stuff set up on the beach for the contest collapsed like a row of dominoes.

I clapped as the huge statue of Reggie toppled over.

Mikey was pretty stoked, too. "Boom chicka-boom, chicka-boom!" he said as he walked away.

Reggie went ballistic. "Don't you walk away from me, Mikey! You'll regret this for the rest of your life. Darn it, Mikey! You're fired!"

His words got drowned out as the statue fell right on top of him. "Uh . . . this is really going to hurt when the shock wears off. . . ."

So much for Reggie.

I know, I know, I haven't finished telling you about Tank.

Well, Lani had saved him, of course, and ever since she'd dragged him onto the beach, he'd been lying in the sand, totally defeated. Next to him now was Chicken Joe's trophy, which the kids had just left lying there.

Suddenly, the trophy grew feet. It righted itself and then waddled past Tank.

Tank blinked. "My lady . . . ," he called. "Wait! It's me! The surfing superstar, Tank, the man, Evans!"

The trophy teetered down the beach. Tank pulled himself up and hurried after it. When he went to lift the thing, Lani's little buddy, Arnold, came tumbling out.

Arnold tried to grab the trophy again.

"Hey! That's not yours!" Tank shouted. "Keep your freaky little hands off my lady!"

Arnold muttered something under his breath.

"Huh?" Tank looked at him, confused. "What did you say?"

Just then Arnold kicked Tank between the legs. Instantly, Tank dropped the trophy and doubled over. Arnold and the rest of the kids piled on top of him. Sand flew everywhere as they pummeled him and kept him pinned to the ground. More and more kids piled on.

"Ahhh!" Tank screamed.

But by then the rest of us were gone. We were at the South Shore, hanging out together, surfing, dancing to music, and having a great old time.

I've got to tell you, dude. The whole thing was a totally sick experience. I mean, going to Pen Gu, meeting Z, surfing Po Chu, starring in a movie . . .

Who would have believed that all of that could happen to me—an ordinary penguin from Shiverpool?

So that's my story.

What's that?

Oh, you're right. It does have a happy ending. Big Z came back, and I got to see my dream come true, even though my brother said it would never happen. Pretty awesome, huh?

Okay, then. If you'll excuse me now, I'm gonna grab my board.

Because you know what they say when the swell's really happening . . .

Surf's up!